THE
NIGHT
THE WATER
CAME

Also by Clive King

ME AND MY MILLION

THE
NIGHT
THE WATER
CAME

Clive King

THOMAS Y. CROWELL   New York

Designed by Joyce Hopkins

Library of Congress Cataloging in Publication Data

King, Clive.
The night the water came.
SUMMARY: A boy who survives a cyclone that destroys
his island home off the coast of Bangladesh is mystified
by the efforts of rescue workers and wants only to return
to his old way of life.
    [1. Cyclones—Fiction. 2. Rescue work—Fiction.
3. Bangladesh—Fiction] I. Title
PZ7.K5754Nh 1982   [Fic]   81–43318
ISBN 0-690-04162-4   AACR2
ISBN 0-690-04163-2 (lib. bdg.)

1 2 3 4 5 6 7 8 9 10
First American Edition

Contents

PRACTICE TAPE

You say if I talk to this machine it will re-member my words? What shall I say to it?

All right, I'll say something. My name is Apu. I live in Kukuri Mukuri Char.

How what? How *old* am I? About eleven years, I think.

I don't understand what you say about birth-days.

Yes, I'd like to hear it say those words back to me.

Was that my voice? It didn't sound like me. Do I talk like that?

You want me to tell you all about the cyclone? But there are lots of things I don't know about it. Why not ask somebody else?

Oh, I see, just the things that happened to me? You'll put it in English and make a *book* about it! Do you think people will be interested? Well, I'm only a boy; I'm not a very important person, am I?

No, I don't mind talking to your machine, if you'll work the switches. I haven't met one like it before, but I've seen so many strange things since the night when my uncle told me to climb the tree that—

Oh, all right, I'll start again properly.

Tape 1:
CYCLONE
STRIKES ISLANDS

It was the middle of the night when my uncle woke me up and told me to climb a tree. I thought he was playing a joke on me, though he's not a person who plays jokes. In fact, he's usually a rather gloomy man and he thinks climbing trees is a waste of time, unless it's to pick coconuts or betel nuts or something useful.

My favorite climbing tree is the big branchy one with the thick trunk that stands near our house. (I mean, it used to stand there. I still can't get used to the idea that it's gone.)

When Uncle woke me it was very dark and I

3

could hear the wind blowing hard and roaring in the branches of the tree. He hurried me outside and I couldn't even see the stars, so the sky must have been covered with clouds. It seemed an odd time to be climbing trees and I started to ask questions, but Uncle told me not to argue and to get climbing.

I know the best way up with my eyes shut. I felt for the low branch above my head, pulled myself up until I could hook my legs over it and hoisted myself up and onto it. I called to Uncle that I was up, and he shouted, "Higher! Higher!" I felt for the branches and stumps that I knew and climbed upward until I was clinging to a thin branch that was tossing and swaying and seemed to be doing its best to throw me off.

The grown-ups were arguing in the darkness below. My uncle was trying to persuade my aunts and cousins to climb up too. I really thought he'd gone crazy like the man in the village on the other side of the island who sometimes sits in the trees like a monkey. (I mean he used to, he's not there any more.) Uncle kept shouting, "The water's coming! The water's coming!" Of course he was right, it did come. I don't know how he knew.

Above the noise of the wind in the branches I could hear some of the words of the argument going on below me. Uncle was shouting, "Up the tree!" Other voices were saying "Not that one," or "To the boats! To the boats!" I shouted down, "Come on, I'll help you!" But of course none of them could climb as well as me: they were either too old or too young. I don't think any of them got into my tree.

The wind tore at me and the branches thrashed about me but I was beginning to see things better. It was still nearly pitch dark but suddenly there was something darker and blacker flying through the air like a huge bat and wrapping itself round the lower branches of my tree. I heard the women's voices wailing, "The roof! The roof!", and I knew it was the thatch of our house going to pieces. I'd seen this happen before. Roofs blow off quite often in the islands. And quite often the water comes up nearly to the top of the mound on which our house is built. But we'd never climbed trees in the middle of the night before.

When the water came it was different from other times. I could hear a roaring of water approaching even above the noise of the wind in the trees and then suddenly it was rushing around the trunk of the tree and pouring over the lower branches. I mean, it didn't rise slowly like the other floods I'd seen; it was halfway up the trunk all at once and I was wet with spray in the highest branches. And then the whole tree seemed to be moving. Yes, I know the branches had been moving but now I had the feeling that everything was slowly toppling, and then I was in the water though I was still holding the branch. And now it was the water instead of the wind that was trying to tear me off the branch, and the rough bark was hurting the skin on my chest and arms as I clung for my life. I struggled and reached for branches above me, caught one and pulled myself clear of the water. There were great salt waves washing over the tree. I could taste them and my eyes stung as I tried to climb above them. The tree was lying right over on its side, and climbing it was quite different. I reached a branch that was clear of the waves and clung on with my arms and legs.

The water didn't seem to be rushing round the trunk as it had been and in the darkness the tops of the other trees seemed to be moving away. Then I knew I was afloat, and alone in the darkness and the storm.

How should I know how long I floated, or how far? All I knew was that I must hang on. Though the current didn't drag at the tree, now that we were floating along with it, the wind still tugged at me and the spray broke over me. The night seemed without end. I even thought that perhaps the sun had been washed away too and it would never return.

I don't know how I got the feeling that I was

always moving through the water, voyaging like a ship through the night. I can only remember the darkness of the sky and the blacker darkness of the waves, but perhaps I did see solid things that stayed still while I moved past them. They must have been the tops of palm trees that were still hanging on to the earth with their roots while the water swirled around them.

Then I think I remember feeling I must be dead or that everything had come to an end, because the wind died down and the waves stopped tearing at me and when I looked up I saw the stars. But all around me was darkness and water and all I could do was lie exhausted on my branch. I was nowhere and there was nothing I could do.

And then it all started again. I thought: *no, there can't be more of it; I can't go on.* But the wind was soon raging again and the waves were once again snatching at me. And somehow I did hold on, though there didn't seem to be any reason why I should. But I must have had enough of my wits about me to notice that I seemed to be going back the way I had come. Perhaps I saw those same palm-tree tops passing the other way—but no, I don't know where I got the feeling that I'd turned round and gone back. Now that I come to think of it, perhaps I never did. But I had this very strong feeling at the time.

By then I suppose I had no hope that the

storm would ever stop or that things would ever be different. But now there came a change in the movement of the tree. Instead of drifting smoothly like a boat, it was bumping and lurching, and I remember thinking: *we've gone aground.* We stuck fast, and now the current was rushing past again, though the wind and waves were not so fierce. And it wasn't so dark. There was the glow in the sky you see before sunrise. Perhaps there was a sun after all!

I think the sun rose, the water drained away, and the wind dropped all about the same time. And there I was.

Where? I was in the tree. The tree was lying on its side among mud and puddles. I had this feeling I was back where I had started, though nothing I could see as the light got stronger looked like the home I knew.

It was a land of mud and battered trees. There was a mound and a creek, but there were no houses on the mound and no boats in the creek. Yet if there *had* been houses on the mound, boats in the creek, more trees here and there, and more branches on the trees that were standing, it could have been home.

Tape 2: SURVIVORS REPORTED

I don't remember doing it, but I must have staggered across to one of the mounds and fallen asleep there. How long did I sleep? I don't know—hours, days, what does it matter? I remember slowly waking up, lying there with my eyes shut, thinking: *I've had a terrible dream, but when I open my eyes I shall see the houses and my family and the cows and the boats as usual.*

I opened my eyes. The dream was real. A warm winter sun was shining, and steam was rising from the muddy, empty fields. There lay my tree, and there were the tracks my feet had left as I walked away from it. There were no other tracks of men, animals, or birds.

Around me stood battered trees that had more or less survived the storm: branching trees with their top branches wrenched off and all their leaves stripped; ragged palm trees, some of them leaning over until they nearly touched the earth. There were holes in the ground, full of water, where trees had been uprooted and carried away. Farther off were the paddy fields where the rice plants lay plastered with mud. There was the empty creek, and beyond it the water of the great river running to the sea, sparkling happily in the sun.

I was lying on a pile of branches and palm leaves on a mound on which the houses must have stood. But the only sign of them was a few bits of palm matting tangled in the branches. And the only sounds were the clicking and snapping of things as they dried in the sun and the murmur of the water as it flowed past the shore. No human voices, no sounds of animals or birds.

I knew I was alive because I was thirsty. I thought there ought to be a well somewhere around, but I couldn't find it. Either I looked in the wrong place or it had got completely choked up with mud and rubbish. So I went down to the shore.

Well, you can't die of thirst on our islands.

You can't always drink the water, of course. When the tide brings the sea water in from the bay you can't drink it, it's too salty. But at the end of the ebb tide it's the river water running past. It's not so clean that you can actually see through it, and I sometimes think it tastes of all the countries and towns it has flowed through, but you can drink it.

After I had drunk I looked out over the water and saw it was full of people. I knew they were dead, of course, and they were too far from the shore for me to see whether they were people I knew. There was nothing I could do for them.

I walked back to the mound again and sat down. My mind was as empty as the island. I had to tell myself who I was. This is what I said to myself:

My name is Apu. Or perhaps that's not my proper name but it's what people call me. The name of my island is Kukuri Mukuri Char. I live there with my uncle Ahmed and my aunties and cousins. My father's name was Bashir, but I don't remember him or my mother because they both disappeared in a boat in a storm soon after I was born. That's what my uncles and aunts always told me. Of course they had to bring me up.

That's all there was to know about me then. Perhaps I was always a little bit different from my cousins because I didn't actually have a father or mother. Perhaps I was a bit more used to looking after myself. Anyway I had to now.

Now I was hungry. The first thing I thought about was the paddy. The rice crop. You can't live without rice, can you? I went to the fields to look at it. Already the plants were beginning to straighten themselves up from the mud, but they didn't look as green and healthy as they should. The grains were not quite ripe but they hadn't fallen off. My uncles would have known whether they were all right or not, and if there was anything that could be done for them. I thought I could pick myself some rice and cook it. Then I remembered that I had no cooking pot, and no fire.

I wandered back to the mound, thinking there must be something left of the kitchen things. But there was nothing, not even a knife. I supposed all the pots had gone floating away on the water but I couldn't understand how the metal things had gone too. They may have just got buried in the mud somewhere, but I never found them. And anyway, how could I light a fire? Usually on the islands we keep a fire going all the time, but if it goes out we have these little sticks with black heads that make fire.

Oh, you know about matches? Well, I didn't have any matches.

In the end I found some roots to eat. You don't eat roots? We do; we sow the seeds in the ground and when the roots grow we eat them. They're better when they're cooked of course but you can eat them without cooking. I found some quite easily near the mound. The leaves were spoiled by the salt water but the roots were all right in the ground. I dug a few up with my fingers and wiped them and ate them.

So there I was with water and food, and sunshine, and the *lungi* I was wearing when I climbed the tree. You don't know what a *lungi* is? Well, it's just a tube of cloth, and you put your legs in and tie it round your middle. Mine was pretty old, and it had got torn in the tree, but it was enough. You don't need much to keep you alive, do you?

It was winter so I didn't expect it would rain anymore—

Oh, you think that sounds funny? It hardly ever rains in our winter. The sky's usually blue and the sun's warm in the daytime. It can be cold at night and it's good to have a fire and a blanket and a roof to protect you from the dew. So I thought I'd better make myself some kind of house. I collected some broken bits of matting from the branches and propped them against the base of a tree. I dried some straw in the sun and made myself a sort of nest to keep me warm.

And so the days passed. How many? It's funny the way people ask me that. I just didn't count the days. Why should I?

The only thing that happened during this time was that the airplanes flew overhead.

Oh, I'm not ignorant, I know about airplanes. Nearly every day you used to be able to see one or two over the islands: shining ones that passed very high and straight, sometimes drawing white lines across the blue sky; fast ones that roared overhead, lower down; winking red lights at night. On the clear nights of winter we'd often see something that looked like a bright star sailing across the sky from one horizon to the other. The older men in the village said they'd never seen such things when they were young and that it was something people had made. But can people make stars?

I had a little cousin who used to wave at airplanes. But then she used to cry for the moon when she was younger. I knew that sort of thing was just childish. Even if all those airplanes had people in them, as I'd been told, it wasn't likely that they'd take any notice of us down there in the islands. And it was no use thinking of reaching for the moon either.

At least, that's what I always thought until the airplane came to our island.

14

I was sitting in the sun, and if I had a thought in my head at all it was to wonder why there weren't even any birds about. I suppose they'd all just been blown away. It was this speck in the sky that made me start thinking about birds, and then the sound of its engine told me it wasn't a bird, but a machine. It made a rather rough, chopping sound as it came over the treetops, quite low down and quite slowly. The noise became louder and louder and then the airplane stopped still in the sky, nearly above me. I didn't know they could do that, though we do have some birds that can.

I thought this thing had great wings flapping above it, but as it hung there I could see they were spinning rather than flapping. It began to come down on me and a great wind came from it that clattered the palm leaves and raised the dust and dead leaves in clouds.

I was frightened. Not so much of the machine as by the wind it made. I had a good reason to be frightened of wind. I ran from the mound, across the paddy field, and hid in the first muddy ditch that I came to. The wind from the machine blew dust and paddy straw over my head.

The noise from the engine stopped. I lifted my head and peered toward it. It was standing among the paddy on four legs and it looked like a glass bottle with four drooping wings above it. I told myself I must be brave and go up to it—

15

anyway, I thought, if it was looking for me it would easily find me.

I crawled out of the ditch and walked toward it, though my legs felt weak under me. As I did so a door opened in the glass bottle and some men got out.

Two of them at least were not like ordinary men. I thought they were looking at me with great metal eyes. Then I thought: *no, they are guns, they have come to kill me.* I was a simple village boy then, you see; I wasn't very sure about foreign men with hair like jute, or about the difference between a gun and a camera. I think I'd seen a man kill a duck with a gun, so I was afraid of these shining things pointed toward me. But there was no loud noise and nothing happened.

The third man, who had black hair like myself, spoke to me in my own language—well, not quite the way we talk in the islands but I could understand what he meant. He asked me questions. The first question was: "What is the name of this island?"

I said, "I am not certain. Is it Kukuri Mukuri Char?"

I could see he pitied me and thought me a very ignorant boy, not even knowing the name of the island I was on.

The next question was: "What is your name?"

I was fairly sure about the answer to that one, so I told him.

Then he asked me who else lived on the island. I still don't know whether I gave the right answer to this question. I began by giving him the name of my uncle Ahmed, and the names of all my other uncles and aunts and cousins, and of the neighbors across the creek. And then I told him about the village on the other side of the island, and told him as many names as I could remember, including the man who used to sit up in the tree. It made me feel better to talk about them like this, and I felt it couldn't be true that they'd all disappeared with the water.

The man spoke to the others in a way I couldn't understand and one of them seemed to be writing it all down on paper. Then he asked me a question that seemed so strange that I took a long time before I answered it. "Do you need food?" he asked.

Did I need food? Was there a clever answer to this one? Who doesn't need food? I've never met anyone who didn't need food. So I thought it was safe to answer yes.

The next question was: "Do you need clothes?" I thought this was even harder. Everybody needs food, but not everybody needs clothes. In the summer my little cousins used to run about naked, and so did the crazy man in the other village sometimes. But most people would say they needed at least one *lungi* to wrap round them, or even two—one to wash and one to wear. And I thought if I said I didn't need clothes he might even take mine away from me, so I answered yes.

He put the next question in a different way. He said: "Is there enough water?" I didn't think it polite to say it was a silly question. *Enough water?* We'd had more than enough. And there was enough water round the island to make it an island. So I said yes, there was enough water.

Then the jute-haired man smiled at me kindly and made me feel I had answered the questions correctly. He said something in his strange speech and the dark-haired man said to me, "Don't worry. The world will hear of this." And they got back into their machine again and the noise started and the wings began to spin again and blow the straw and dust about. And I was frightened of the wind it made and ran and hid in the ditch again. The airplane went up into the air and moved quickly away.

Then a thought came to me. *If I had asked the men for a box of matches, would they have given me one?* But it was too late now.

The wind of the machine had blown away my roof of matting and my straw bed, and it took some time to gather it all up again. Then I gave myself a supper of cold radish and settled down for another lonely night with the saying in my head: "The world will hear of this." What could it mean? Had I done right or wrong?

Tape 3:
AIRDROP

You, too, may be thinking that I was very stupid not to know whether I was on my own island or not. But our islands are all much the same, except for their shape. And their shapes are always changing.

Somebody told me once that there are places in the world where the earth is piled up in great heaps, higher than the tallest trees. This may be true, though I've never seen it. They even said that the earth reaches up into the clouds—but you don't have to believe everything you're told. All I know is that the water rises and falls, and the land is usually a little bit above it. In some places the mudbanks rise slowly out of the water until grass or rice can grow on them. A new island like this we call a *char*. In other places the current eats away the steep banks, and trees and even houses fall into the water.

To keep above the water we build mounds of earth and on each of these we build a *bari*. You don't know the word? A *bari* isn't a house, and it isn't a village, though it *is* a home. It's a cluster of huts on one mound, and everybody who lives there is uncle or aunt or cousin to everybody else.

Well, this is how it used to be on Kukuri Mukuri Char and on all the other islands I'd ever heard about. But on that terrible night the water must have gone right over the island, right over the mounds, and carried all the *baris* away. And all that was left was the flat fields and empty mounds, a shoreline that had crumbled away and creeks that were choked with mud. There was only myself to say whether it was Kukuri Mukuri Char or not, and I couldn't be sure.

When you are living like a mouse in a hole and scratching for your food, one day is the same as another. I don't know how many days passed before the airplane came back.

It's come back was what I thought at first. Then I thought: *it'll blow away my roof and my straw again;*

I'd better stay and hang on to them. My next thought was: *either it can change its shape or it's something different.* Its sound wasn't the chopping noise and it wasn't the bottle with the thin wings spinning above it. It was a great tin shed with stiff arms on each side.

It didn't stop in the air but flew over very fast and very low, then it turned round and flew back again even lower. It seemed to be just over the tops of the palm trees. Its noise was louder than thunder and I was afraid that the wind would come again, but it didn't. It turned again, and I could see a great door open in the side of it. I could even see a man standing inside the door.

It flew round once again and came toward me over the treetops. I crept into my nest, where I felt safer. As it roared overhead I saw things falling from it, and I remembered talk I'd heard, among my uncles, of how airplanes were used to drop things on people and kill them. I was very much afraid again. This was worse than the wind of the other machine, worse than the shining things that the men had pointed at me.

The things fell very quickly from the airplane and landed with a thump in the paddy field. I didn't know whether they had been meant to fall on my little house with me in it. It was bad enough that they crushed the growing rice plants.

Three times the airplane flew back and forth and dropped things. Many of them fell among the paddy, others crashed into the trees and bushes. I cowered under my matting roof, but I suppose it wouldn't have saved me if something had dropped on it. For some reason—something I'd heard from my uncles, I suppose—I expected these things to make fire and loud noises, but they only thumped onto the ground and bounced a bit. Then the airplane flew away. I thought I saw the man inside the door shaking his fist or waving his hand. I wasn't sure which.

It was a long time before I dared to look closely at the things that had fallen. From a distance they seemed to be of different kinds. Well, some looked hard and some looked softer. One big square box had burst open and metal things had spilled out.

As last I decided that they weren't going to burst into flames, so I went up to one of them. It was a great bundle done up in sacking and held together with very strong bands of black metal. It was much too heavy for me to lift, and anyway I didn't think I ought to move it. I went over to the big broken box and looked at the metal things that had spilled out. They had signs on them, some kind of writing, and pictures of cows—

Look, we're not completely ignorant down in

the islands! I'd heard of keeping food in tins and I did wonder if these tins with cows on them had cowmeat in them. But then some of the other tins had pictures of babies on them, and I didn't like to think what they might have inside—I mean, we're not cannibals! Why didn't I open them? What with? I know how tins are opened now, but then I didn't, and anyway there wasn't even a knife on the island. Hard stones? Oh yes, I've been told about places where hard things grow in the earth, but I've never actually seen them.

Anyhow, what I was really worried about was the real food, the paddy crop. Here were all these things lying about all over it, stopping it growing. I thought nobody would mind if I moved the bales and boxes to the side of the field. They'd be able to find them if they came to look for them. First I carried away the small tins and stacked them up. Then I found that by rolling the big boxes end over end I could just move these too. I hoped I wasn't doing more damage to the paddy by rolling things over it than by leaving them there. My uncles would very soon have told me if they'd been there but I had to decide these things for myself.

Then I thought I might borrow the big broken box as a roof to my house. I felt quite proud of it the first night I slept under it and I think it kept me warmer. And during the next two days

I managed to roll the big bales and boxes up onto the mound and build them into walls for my house. As I sat and munched my radishes I thought at least I was looking after these things until somebody came for them.

Tape 4:
NAVY LANDS
MARINES

You do get tired of living on roots and water. I felt a longing for fish, and if I'd had a net I could have tried to catch some. But of course I still had nothing to cook them with and raw fish is worse than raw roots.

I used to sit on the bank looking out over the water. Usually you can see a lot of fishing boats from our island but they, too, seemed to have vanished. I really thought at that time that, apart from the airplanes that stay in the sky, all the world had been drowned. An old aunt used to tell me a story of how this had happened once and I supposed it could have happened again.

But one day I saw a boat far out toward the open sea. No, it was two boats, three boats! So not all the fishermen had disappeared. They were moving very fast though, not the way our country boats move when the boatmen paddle them or punt them with long bamboos or sail them under their square sails. Then I heard a sound of engines and I thought: *an airplane, too.* I looked up into the sky, but there was nothing. The noise was coming from the boats. Oh yes, I'd seen motorboats, though I can't remember one ever coming to our island and actually stopping.

The boats came along: one, two, three, like ducks in a line. When they came nearer I could see that they didn't look like our country boats at all. They didn't have the long curved beaks and sterns our boats have, nor houses on them. They looked like square boxes floating.

They came in from the sea, following the channel of deep water that I knew ran close to the shore of our island. There was a man standing up in the first boat pointing a pair of big glass eyes at me. They flashed in the sun. The man waved his arm and all three boats suddenly turned and came straight toward the shore where I was standing. I could see a number of big men standing in each of the boats, all dressed the same in mud-colored clothes, and something put into my head the word: soldiers.

I'd never seen soldiers, only heard about them, but I felt afraid again. I thought: *they've come to fight, or take me prisoner.* Wasn't that what soldiers did? So I ran away.

It's difficult to hide on our island. I ran until I came to a ditch, and crouched down in it. When I peeped out through a clump of reeds I could see the enemy spreading out in a long line and walking toward me over the paddy fields. I could see that things weren't too easy for them either. Every now and then they would come to a ditch and they'd have to jump over it or wade through it. I ran along the side of my ditch, keeping my head down. I thought I might be able to get round the end of their line. When I looked up over the edge of the ditch again there was a soldier a few yards away. I think he was as startled as I was. I plunged through the ditch, over my knees in water and mud, and climbed out on the other side. The soldier shouted at me, but when I looked back he didn't seem to be in a hurry to get after me.

I ran and hid in a clump of trees around an-other *bari* mound, covering myself with fallen palm leaves. When I looked out again I could see the soldiers were still coming slowly after me, search-ing all the ditches and bushes as they came. They

28

got nearer and I slipped out behind the mound and ran again. Again they shouted at me and came slowly on.

Although I wasn't feeling very strong after living on roots for all those days I felt I could have kept ahead of those soldiers if they hadn't cornered me on a point of land with the shore on one side and a big creek on the other. I didn't feel strong enough to swim the creek so I just squatted there and let the soldiers come up to me.

Two of them stood and looked down at me, and I wondered what they would do. They both had pink faces and one of them had eyes the color of the sky, which looked very strange. They said some words I didn't understand, then one of them took me by the arm. He was quite gentle about it but I thought: *now I'm a prisoner.*

There was a lot of blowing of whistles and shouting, and all the soldiers seemed to be gathering at my *bari* where I'd stacked the boxes. I knew they would soon find them and I supposed they would take them away with them. They led me back to my little house of boxes, and I wondered: *will they think I stole it all?* But they just looked at me and all the unopened boxes and seemed puzzled, not angry.

They made signs like eating, putting their

29

hands to their mouths and pointing to the boxes. I couldn't understand what they wanted, then I thought: *perhaps they're hungry.* I searched among the straw of my bed and found a radish that I'd been keeping for supper, and offered it to them. I suppose one radish wasn't much among all those soldiers, though it was quite a lot to me. Some of them laughed, but some of them seemed almost to be crying.

Then one of them took a folding knife from his pocket and opened a little hooked blade. He dug this into one of the tins, cut the top off, and handed it to me. It had white sticky stuff inside it and I wasn't sure what to do with it, but the soldier put his finger into it and licked it, and I did the same.

It was the sweetest stuff I'd ever tasted, and after all those radishes of course it was delicious. They made me eat the whole tin.

Then I ran behind a tree and was sick.

After some more talk which I didn't understand, the soldiers led me toward the boats. I didn't want to be taken away from my home but I was too weak and sick to resist. The boats had square doors in the front that let down like flaps and they led me across one of these. The water had risen and the boats floated away quite easily. Then with a sudden roar that made me jump they started the engine. We went backward away from the shore, turned together with the other boats and headed for the sea. I thought: *they're taking me far over the sea to a distant country and I shall never see my home again.* For the first time since the great storm, I cried.

I suppose I'd been expecting a long voyage over the sea in the square boat, days and weeks perhaps, but the sun hadn't moved very far in the sky when I saw we were approaching something that seemed to be standing in the middle of the sea. I supposed it must be some kind of ship, but the closer we got to it the less it looked like any kind of ship I'd ever seen or heard of.

It was—what? A huge tin shed with a flat top built on the water. A great house, the size of hundreds of houses, black against the sun on the silver waves. A prison perhaps. I'd heard of prisons. There were little square boats coming and going all round it. And on top—you may not believe this—on the flat top there were airplanes sitting.

The boat stopped at a great ladder by the side of the ship. This time I didn't want to leave the boat, but they made me get onto the ladder and walk up to a big opening high above the water. There were men in very clean blue and white clothes at the top. We went through a door, and

31

I was inside the prison of metal. Everything was white, and there were pipes like palm trunks everywhere, and in my ears there was all the time a great humming sound as if monstrous insects were imprisoned in this metal box.

In a way I was more frightened than when I was alone in the tree with the water and the wind. I had no idea what they were going to do with me. Was I to be shut up for ever here away from the sun? They took me down long, bright tunnels with these white snakes above my head and smooth brown floors under my feet, through thick iron doors, then they pushed me through a door into a place full of pipes and shining troughs.

And then they took my clothes from me and left me naked! I know my *lungi* was very old and torn and dirty, but it was the only one I had and I didn't see what right they had to steal it. They gave me soap—oh, I know soap when I see it, we're not as ignorant as all that—pushed me into an enclosed space, and suddenly there was water falling on me.

That was a shock of course. Next to wind, a sudden rush of water is one of the things I like least. I cried out at first. But I'm not a fool. I could understand that they wanted me to wash. Yes, we do wash. My uncle used to make me wash at least once a day. Perhaps since I'd been living alone I hadn't been washing so often, and I was ashamed to see how dirty I was. Once I started washing with the beautiful soap and the warm water that appeared so magically from above me I could hardly stop, but they pulled me out and gave me a lovely soft white robe to wrap myself in. I tied it round me, but the man pulled it away from me, rubbed me dry with it and threw it on the damp floor as if it was nothing. Then they brought me clothes—what I would call a pant and a shirt—of fine white cloth. They gave me a comb to comb my hair and showed me a great mirror on the wall. When I looked at this clean brown boy in the white shirt and pant I wondered who it was. It couldn't be Apu of Kukuri Mukuri Char, but perhaps it was somebody who fitted in better with the metal prison with the white pipes and the humming.

When I was dressed they took me through more doors and—perhaps you won't believe this either—they took all my new clothes off me again! Just as I was beginning to feel part of the white metal world I was once again naked and nothing.

I'm afraid I cried again. A man with glasses on his nose looked at me with a worried expression and said something to another man, who went out and came back with a glass of milk. It wasn't the thick sticky stuff that had made me sick, and it wasn't the good milk we get from our cows and buffaloes either. But I drank it and felt a little better, though I was still naked.

They did some rather frightening things to me then. The man with the glasses felt me and looked at me all over: my eyes, ears, teeth, hair, skin—yes, everything. He looked at the scratches I'd got from clinging to the tree, and the other man put grease on them and covered them with something that stuck to my skin. The glasses man shone lights into my eyes and mouth and put a cold tube on my chest. He scratched the soles of my feet and hit me on the knee with a hammer. They stuck a pin into my thunb and took blood from me, and I had to fill up a little pot with my own water. Then they came at me with a needle and stuck it into my arm. I was determined not to cry again, and actually for all their instruments of torture they hardly succeeded in hurting me at all.

What do you say? You're used to having all these things done to you? Oh, well, I won't go on about them then. But, you see, I still didn't know whether these people were friends or enemies, or what they were going to do with me.

They gave me back my fine new clothes and took me to a place where there were people sitting among a lot of papers, and one of them was one of our people. I mean he didn't have strange-colored hair and eyes and he spoke my language—not very well though; we didn't always understand each other. He told me to sit down on a chair, then he asked me a lot of questions. I didn't feel at all sure about the answers, sitting there on a chair in this metal prison surrounded by humming. The questions and my answers went something like this:

"What is your name?"

"Apu."

(He wrote it on the paper.)

"But it's not my real name," I added.

(He crossed it out.)

"What's your real name?"

"Anisuzzaman—I think."

(He started to write it down, then stopped.)

"You think? Aren't you sure?"

(It was a long time since I'd used it. It sounded strange.)

"I think I'm sure."

(He wrote it down, rather doubtfully.)

"Where is your *bari*?"

"I don't know."

(It had been washed away. How should I know where it was?)

"Where is your family?"

"I don't know."

"Where were you on the night of the cyclone?"
"What is cyclone?"

(I had to ask. I'd never heard the word before.)
"A cyclone is a circular wind," he explained.
"I don't think I ever saw one," I said.

(What would a circular wind look like?)
"Where were you when the boats picked you up?"
"On Kukuri Mukuri Char—I think."

(He had started writing again, then stopped.)
"Don't you know?"
"It doesn't look the same. Perhaps it isn't."
"How many people need food?"

(That odd question again! But I thought I knew the answer.)
"Sir, everybody needs food."
"Have you enough clothes?"
"Yes, I have a shirt and a pant."
"Is there anything else you need?"
"Yes, a box of matches."

(He wrote it down.)
"How are the crops?"

(At last, a sensible question!)
"Sir," I said, "the paddy is still standing and the grain is in the ear. But the airplanes drop things on it and the soldiers walk all over it."

He looked at me strangely. "The airplanes and the soldiers are there to help you," he said.

(All those airplanes and soldiers just to help me? I couldn't believe it.)

36

The man looked at what he had written on the paper, shrugged his shoulders, screwed it up into a little ball and threw it toward a basket standing on the floor. It missed, so I got down off my chair and helped it into the basket, where some other writings were kept. Then he felt in his pockets and handed me a box of matches.

"Don't worry, you'll be looked after," he said. "You can go now."

I suppose I should have asked where, but I just wandered out into the humming tunnels. That place still comes back to me in my dreams, and sometimes I wonder if I didn't dream it to begin with. I passed men carrying papers and men carrying pots of paint. They were all rather surprised to see me but seemed too busy to ask me where I was going. I looked into a dark room and saw— I still haven't got words to tell you what I saw. There seemed to be machines with wheels and tapes like this one I'm talking to, and great round things shaped like the watches people wear on their wrists, but huge and glowing like the moon in the dark. I went down ladders, because I thought the sea must be down there somewhere, and saw a great space full of what I suppose were machines, but so huge that the men who moved among them looked smaller than the little birds that perch on the water buffaloes. Some of these machines spun and hummed, and some were silent. These great shapes frightened me, so I climbed back up the endless iron ladders until I came to—well, a room full of airplanes. They were like the one that had come down onto my island and had seemed so big and frightening in the sky, but here they were, a number of them in their own *bari,* and men in blue clothes were washing them as we wash our cows. Others seemed to be building them, just as we put together bamboos to make our houses.

These men in blue looked at me in surprise too, and then went on with their work. I stood beside one of these machines and then—I can only tell this story as I remember it and this is what I think happened next—as I stood there bells began to ring and then the whole floor we were on started to move upward, carrying the machines and the men and myself toward a great bright opening in the roof. And there we were in the sunlight on a great flat island. There were more airplanes standing on the rest of the island, but what I was glad to see was the blue sky and the sparkling sea all around.

When the floor I was standing on stopped moving I walked to the edge of the island and looked down. I had never been so high above the water and it made me dizzy, but I saw one thing that comforted me. The ship I was on—somehow I knew it must be a ship as well as a prison and an island—the ship had a great chain leading from one end into the water. Each link of the chain looked the size of my arm, but I know boats and I thought it must be the monstrous chain for a monstrous anchor. Where the chain dipped into the water was the thing I was glad to see. It was one of our own country boats full of our own island people—the first of my own people I had seen for days, since the night in the tree.

They were shouting to the men on the great ship, who were shouting angrily back at them. I couldn't understand what was happening, but my one thought was that I must get back to my own people. I couldn't wander about in this strange metal world for ever.

I don't know how I managed it but I found my way down ladders and along tunnels to where the great iron chain began. I crawled through the hole where it left the ship and, hanging upside down from the great links, with the foaming sea beneath my head, I climbed down it toward the wooden boat.

They were shouting at me from both sides, from the great ship in their strange language and from the country boat in mine. Everyone seemed angry with me, but I was glad even to be scolded in the island language.

I dropped off the chain onto the boat, and

the first thing they said to me was "What did you get from them?" I looked at my new clothes and saw that they weren't clean and white any more, but smeared with rust and mud from the anchor chain.

"They gave me a shirt and a pant," I said. "And a box of matches."

They pushed me into the deck house of the boat, and they took my new clothes off me! My own people did that to me! I screamed and cursed at them, but they stripped me and gave me a *lungi* in exchange. It was even older and more torn than the one I'd left on the ship.

One of the men called from the deck house to the person who seemed to be doing the most shouting on the deck: "O Abdurrahman! He has nothing in his pockets."

Abdurrahman came in. He was a strong, rough man with a thick, black beard and I was afraid of him after the treatment his men had given me already, but he spoke to me quite cheerily.

"You might have filled your pockets at least," he said. "But tell me how you got on board?"

I told him how the soldiers had caught me on the island. He asked about my family and I told him everything about the storm and how I'd lived on radishes. At least he seemed to understand, and it was good to be able to speak in my

40

own tongue. When I told about the things the airplanes had dropped he began to get interested. He wanted to know if the things were still there and I said I thought they were. Immediately he shouted orders to his crew and they stopped clinging to the anchor chain and pushed off.

The strong current caught the boat and swept it toward some of the white painted boats tied alongside the ship. One of our men took the broad-bladed steering oar and tried to steer us clear but we collided with one of the beautiful boats. A sailor on it pushed us off, using a pole with a hook on it and a lot of strong language—I didn't understand the words but they didn't sound friendly. Then we dropped astern of the great ship and were carried toward the islands by the flooding tide.

All this time Abdurrahman was either shouting or laughing. I could see he was a sailor and not a farmer. The water people are usually jollier than people like my uncles who grow rice. As some of the men took the long rowing oars in the bows, and another sculled and steered with the great stern oar, Abdurrahman talked to me and I began to be less afraid of him.

"They know us too well on that ship," he said. "The first time we took the boat out there they loaded us with food and clothing and didn't ask questions. The second time we pretended to be another crew and we got as much again. The third time they recognized us, but we said we were collecting goods for starving families on a distant island. They made us sign papers with our thumbprints and told us not to come back again. This time we were trying to persuade them to pay us to transport goods ashore, but they got angry with us. Never mind, we've not done badly. We'll try somewhere else. If you can lead us to the loot, you can join us. But we can't have you looking well clothed and well fed, can we?"

I understood now that they'd taken my new clothes away so that people would be sorry for me in my old *lungi*. Then I said, "I'm not well fed. They gave me one tin of milk that made me sick and a glass of milk that didn't."

I thought he would be sorry for me but he only sniffed. "You'll have to do better than that if you work for us. One shirt, one pant and some milk, after all that! All those soldiers and ships and airplanes are there to help us, you know."

"That's what the man in the ship said," I told him. "But I didn't believe it."

"Ah, it's hard enough to believe," said Abdurrahman. "But it seems that the great storm has turned the world upside down. It has drowned our people and sunk our boats and killed our cat-

42

tle, but it has also driven the foreigners crazy. Instead of taking our goods from us and making us poor, which is the natural way of things, they are giving things away. A lot of it is things we don't want, like tasteless food fit only for sick babies, but they're also giving away good rice and cloth and blankets that fetch a high price on the market. Why they are doing so passes my understanding, but it's happening all over the islands and the coast. Since they say it's for us I intend to get as much as I can while the madness lasts."

During the long pull back to the coast they cooked a meal. It was real food! Plenty of fine white rice, spices and hot chillies, vegetables, fish. It took a long time for them to prepare it, in front of my eyes in the deck house, and my empty stomach complained loudly of the delay. But it was worth waiting for. At last it was cooked to the taste of Abdurrahman and I was allowed to join the others, cramming handfuls of the mixture into my mouth. This was what my stomach had been craving for all those days. Even if I had fallen among pirates, as Abdurrahman's way of talking made me believe, there was a lot to be said for the pirates' way of life.

The sun was falling toward the sea to the west and the islands were low gray shapes to the north. Abdurrahman took me onto the pointed prow of the boat and asked me which island was mine. I realized that I was not a sailor, and wondered how they found their way about the islands where the only landmarks were leafy trees and palm trees. And now even these were so battered by the storm that they looked quite different from what they had been.

Two members of the crew claimed to know Kukuri Mukuri Char and a fierce discussion flowed about currents and sandbanks and depths. They prodded the bottom with long bamboos, they examined the mud that came up on the end of them. They even dipped up some water in a bucket on a line and tasted it, and had an argument about the taste. But I think it was more by luck than good navigation that late in the afternoon we came to a stretch of shore that I recognized mainly by the marks left by the soldiers' boats that morning.

They beached the boat and I jumped ashore with Abdurrahman, and led him toward my *bari*. Proudly I showed him the stack of boxes and bales.

"Are you sure these are all meant for me?" I asked.

He kicked rather contemptuously at the bales. "Not as much as I expected, but a lot too much for a little boy," he said. "Let's see what's in them."

Some of the men got busy trying to open the bales. It was quite difficult for them, even with their strong knives, to break the metal bands that held them together. They started ripping the sacking covers off and taking out the dozens of blankets inside, but Abdurrahman stopped them angrily. He ordered them to pick up the bales and boxes and take them back to the boat. He only laughed when I asked whether it wouldn't be better to leave some of them there in case my family came back. It was only then that I saw he just meant to steal them.

"I thought you said these things were for me," I protested.

"Nothing of the sort," he laughed. "I said they were for us."

I trotted unhappily after the men as they carried the goods to the boat. "You're thieves!" I shouted at them. "Pirates! Dacoits!" They only laughed.

When they reached the shore they heaved the boxes and bales onto the boat. Abdurrahman turned to me, grinning.

"Well," he said. "Are you joining my band of thieves and pirates and dacoits, or not?"

"No!" I shouted. "Give me my things back!"

"Please yourself," he said, and jumped into the boat with the others. They began to push off with the bamboo poles.

"Give me my shirt and pant!" I shouted, trying

45

to keep back my tears. They laughed louder as the boat moved away from the bank.

"At least give me my box of matches!" I wept. "It's in my pant pocket." I'd only just remembered it. I think it was the cook who took pity on me. He was an old man with a white beard. As the boat moved swiftly backward the matchbox came flying through the air toward me, and landed in a muddy puddle on the shore.

I was going to leave it there, but even then I thought: *there's always tomorrow; they'll dry in the sun.* So I fished it out.

I stood and watched the pirate vessel. The square red sail was raised to catch the evening breeze and then it drew smoothly away from the island.

I walked back to my *bari*. Dusk was falling. I was alone again, and no better off than I'd been before the soldiers came.

Yes I was! I still had my box roof and my straw. There was the sacking from one of the bales. I could wrap it round me like a blanket. And there was some of the hard metal strip that had held the bale together. Where it was broken it had a sharp edge; perhaps I could use it as a knife. I had my sodden matchbox. I opened it carefully and saw that there were only about a dozen matches in it, but I thought I could save them.

46

And then I had a stroke of luck. Hidden among the straw of my bed I found one of the tins. I thought that perhaps tomorrow I could open it with a piece of the metal strip, and eat it slowly. I could keep going. And meanwhile I'd at least had a good meal out of the pirates.

Tape 5:
RUBBER BOATS
LAND
RELIEF GOODS

I was lonelier and hungrier than ever when I woke up next morning. I'd had one good meal and it had given me an appetite; I'd met people and I felt the need for company. It was difficult to go back to just keeping alive, but I had to.

I remembered my matches, and I took them and stuck them in a patch of bare earth in a row like soldiers. *Perhaps the soldiers will come back,* I thought as I did it. I wouldn't run away from them again, in spite of their jute hair and red faces and sky-blue eyes. I took my tin of milk and a piece of metal strip, and tried to open the tin. The metal slipped and cut my finger a little. I tied my finger up with a leaf and tried again. By boring away carefully in one place I managed after a long time to make a hole through the tin so that I could suck the sweet milk through. There was no danger of eating too much, too quickly. I could only suck a little at a time. But there was plenty of time. I took the tin down to the shore so that I could keep a lookout over the water, in case the boats came back.

I was so busy looking out toward the south, where the boats had appeared the day before, that it was a shock when I happened to look the other way and saw that they had sneaked up on me from the north.

But they weren't the same. They weren't the square-ended boats that had butted their way through the waves yesterday. There were four of them and they came toward me with wings of white spray on each side of them. In the channel by the island there were little short waves, and these boats came leaping and dancing over them like the young calves that leap and jump before they become staid old cows.

The first two roared and bounced past the shore where I was standing. They were quite small boats, black and orange in color, and in each of them I could see two men crouching, and some boxes and bundles. The men in the first two waved but did not stop. Then I thought: *the soldiers and the airplanes and the boats are there to help me.* Perhaps even these strange bouncing boats were, too. So as the second pair came leaping by I waved and shouted as loud as I could—and one of them swirled round in a great shower of spray and headed for the beach. The fourth one stopped its engine and waited in the water.

As the boat came to the shore I was thinking: *what's the use, they'll be strangers who don't understand my language.* The person who leapt ashore first was quite a young man in clothes like a soldier, with a green scarf round his neck. He greeted me in my own language and I didn't wait for him to ask difficult questions. I said: "I'm all alone on this island and I've got one tin of milk and twelve matches." The young man spoke with the other man in the boat, who was in a bright yellow garment, and then said, "All right, jump in!"

So I jumped. Treading on the side of the boat was like treading on the belly of a buffalo, it was round and soft and bouncy. The man in yellow pulled a string from the machine at the back of the boat and it began to roar. We went backward for a bit then shot forward, bumping and smacking over the waves so that I had to hold on to the ropes fixed to the skin of the boat to stay in it at all.

"Are you hungry?" shouted the young man. I nodded. He opened a huge square tin and gave me a handful of biscuits (though I didn't know the word biscuit then). I almost choked on them as we jumped a wave and landed smack on the water the other side. They thumped me on the back and we all laughed.

The young man looked at the sackcloth which I was still wearing and said, "Do you want some clothes?" I nodded again with my mouth full of biscuit, and he took from the pile of goods that filled the boat a strange bag that you could see through like glass. It was full of clothes, all in bright colors. He pulled out a pair of trousers and measured them against me, then told me to put them on. I let go of the rope I was hanging on to and tried to pull on these trousers under my *lungi*. The boat gave a flop like a porpoise and I fell backward over the side. The man in yellow grabbed me by the ankle at the last moment and hauled me back. We were all roaring with laughter; you couldn't help it in the bouncing boat. I struggled into the blue trousers while they held me by the arms, then they handed me a red shirt and held me by the legs. At the same time they gave me another handful of biscuits and I got so confused with the shirt and the biscuits that I really did choke this time, and they had to give me some water out of a strange soft see-through bottle. Of

51

course I spilt most of the water down my neck and at the same time a wave broke over the front of the boat and wetted us all. I coughed and spluttered and wiped myself and laughed till I cried. I had no idea where I was going or how this crazy journey would end. They gave me a green garment with a strange device on it that sewed me up the front in no time at all, and when the sea broke over me again the water ran off as if I was a duck. Then they found a black thing with a beak to it and put it on my head. They threw the sackcloth and my *lungi* over the side and they laughed so much at me in my new clothes that I wished I could see what I looked like.

We had caught up with the two other boats by now, and we followed them round a point of land into the mouth of a river. The waves ceased and the boats stopped bouncing.

And we stopped laughing.

The bank on the south of the river was covered with the bodies of buffaloes, cows, and goats. And the bodies of people. I knew I was fortunate to be alive.

I could see *bari* mounds swept bare of buildings, but on one of them there was matting and palm fronds propped up against a tree to make a shelter like the one I had made for myself. I pointed it out, because nobody seemed to have noticed it. The man in yellow shouted to the other boats and they all slowed down and turned toward the shore.

We landed where the bodies were. I wasn't as much afraid of them as I'd expected to be. I felt their souls had gone to paradise long ago.

You do know about souls, don't you?

Some men came from among the trees. They told us that many people had been carried away by the water, but there were some people in the shelters. The men from the boats talked for a while, then one of them turned to me and said, "The women won't allow strange men to see them, but you're a boy; you can go in."

I went into the shack. There were two women lying on some straw, one of them holding a very small baby. I greeted them and said, "How is your baby, Auntie?" (Of course she wasn't my auntie, that's just the way we talk.)

"The baby has no milk."

I went out and told the boat people. Somebody went back to the boats and fetched a box and a bundle. They opened the box and took out a big tin. They called for a clean bowl and showed the men how to mix the powder from the tin with water to make milk. They used water from the bottle in the boat, which they said was clean. I took the bowl in to the women and they fed the little baby with a spoon. Then I gave them some cloth for the women and the baby to wear, and we left them the big tin of powder.

How foolish I am, I thought. *I feel like crying again, but this is nothing to be sad about. These people need help, and we can help them.* I began to understand now what the airplanes and the soldiers and people were doing all over the islands.

I said goodbye to the women and they called out, "Blessings on you, *sahib!*"

Sahib? I looked round to see who they were talking to, but there was only me in the shack. You only say *sahib* to a gentleman, somebody of importance. Then I realized it was me, Apu of Kukuri Mukuri, who had been living on radishes and river water myself a few days ago, that they were addressing so respectfully. Or rather I knew it was the blue trousers and the red shirt and the green jacket and the black hat that made me one of the people who helped, instead of one of the people who had to be helped.

We handed out some blankets and clothes for the men too, then got back into the boats and continued our journey up the river. The further up the river we went the more people there were on the banks, including young children and even dogs. The water can't have been very deep here, if even the dogs escaped. The two other boats had gone on ahead while we were helping the family, and their crews had got a whole village lined up near the shore. We beached the boats and landed the boxes and bundles. The young men with the green scarves began to hand out lengths of cloth and blankets and biscuits, and tins of food for the children, moving down the lines as the people squatted and waited patiently. I wondered if I should join one of the lines and get my blanket and my tin of food, but when I tried to the villagers got angry and pushed me away. I thought: *it's all very well being a sahib, but where do I belong and how shall I live?* The people in this village didn't want me and I couldn't go back to my island alone.

Then they began to open the see-through sacks of fine clothes and hand them out. There were gay shirts, and coats of wool and of the fur of animals, and beautiful hats, and garments of such strange shapes and sizes that nobody knew what to make of them. The head man of the village was of course the first to receive them and when he couldn't make up his mind whether to put his arms or his legs into a curious pink garment everyone laughed at him and he became angry. He said all the bags should go to him, and he would hand them out later, and then the other men protested and said he would keep them for himself.

I heard a man muttering near me: "They sell

these things to the *sahibs* in the towns for many rupees." The men began to leave their lines and snatch at the rich clothes, pushing and pulling each other to get at them. The crews of the boats were surrounded by a struggling mob, and somebody even tried to pull my clothes off me, but I'd had enough of that. I pushed my way through to where the boats' crews were now hitting about with their flat paddles to keep the crowds from the boats. We jumped aboard and pushed off, leaving the villagers to their squabbles. Nobody had invited me into the boats but they seemed to accept me as belonging to them and not to the village.

The four boats raced back down the river, swirling round the corners and building up great waves with their wash, then we were out into the choppy sea and bouncing worse than ever against the wind. Our boat was like a bull stung by an insect, bucking and rearing and trying to shake us out. After quite a long time of this, during which I still had no chance to wonder where we were going or what lay at the end of my journey, we got into calmer water and there ahead of us was a big vessel lying some distance from the shore.

As we got closer I could see it wasn't exactly a country boat like Abdurrahman's, nor was it a huge metal island with airplanes on top of it. I think I'd seen ones like it before, it was a big wooden river launch on which hundreds of people travel from place to place. Clustered round it like black-and-orange bees were more of the bouncing boats.

We tied up alongside and climbed on board. I was glad to find it was not a clanging, humming, white-painted world but rather a muddle of bits of boats, wooden beams and coils of rope, spare machines like those on the back of the boats, and boxes and bales of goods. And it was full of people, some talking my language and some talking in other tongues. They all wore clothes like the ones I was wearing, though mostly older and dirtier. People smiled at me and said hullo, but nobody seemed to think I was anything very strange. So I didn't feel too strange myself.

They took me up wooden ladders to a place where there was a good smell of food. There was a young boy about my age, dressed in a *lungi*, helping with the food. He looked at my clothes and spoke to me respectfully. Someone handed me a plate piled with food and my mouth began to water—I'd only had a few biscuits since my meal with the pirates the day before. I was about to take a handful of the food and fill my mouth with it when the young boy snatched the plate away.

This was too much! I was about to attack him when he said, "Do you eat the forbidden meat?"

The forbidden meat! I was horrified. I saw some of the pink-faced men standing around eating the pink slices and couldn't believe I was surrounded by pig-eaters. But the young boy just laughed and got me another plate piled with rice and curry. My appetite soon recovered from the shock and I had my second good meal in as many days. It's odd what strange surroundings you can get used to when you have to.

Tape 6:
MINISTER FLIES TO AFFECTED AREAS

Looking back I can hardly believe all these things happened in one day. But my life after the night in the tree was like that: either sitting alone on an empty island eating roots, or moving in worlds I never dreamed of.

The people on the launch were finishing their meal when there were shouts of "Airplane! Airplane!", and the sound of engines overhead. We climbed onto the flat top of the launch and waved to the airplane circling in the sky. Then it began to come down. It didn't hang in the sky and then drop like the first one that came to the island,

and it didn't roar overhead like the second one. It glided gently toward the water like a big waterbird, skimmed along the surface sending up a stream of spray, settled, and stopped. Somebody quickly got into one of the little boats alongside, started the engine, and zoomed toward the plane resting on the sea, and soon it was coming back with more people in it.

We went below in the ship to see who these visitors were. The first to come on board had a pink face and jute hair that was rather long. The next was a dark man who somehow looked rather important. As they shook hands with the people on the ship I couldn't help staring at the first man, and I noticed that the ship's crew were staring too. The young boy who helped with the food was beside me and I whispered to him, "What a strange man!"

He giggled and whispered back, "He's a woman." I saw now that this was true, but she was the first woman I'd seen who wore trousers like a man.

There was a great deal of talk in different languages. The important-looking man asked a lot of questions and looked at papers stuck up on a board and made a speech in the language I didn't understand. Then he made a speech in our language and told us that thousands of people were hungry and naked and homeless because of the cyclone. I began to understand that cyclone was something to do with my night in the tree. He told us what good work we were doing by helping them. I thought of how I'd given milk food to the woman with the baby and once again felt quite proud and useful.

Then somebody said, "We have a problem here," and pushed me forward. I wished they hadn't. Now I was a problem. I thought: *they're going to ask me difficult questions again, like "Do people need food?"* I was glad when somebody else explained, in my language, that I was the only survivor on my island and they didn't know what to do with me. The important man asked me if I had any relations, or belongings on the island. I said, "Half a tin of milk and twelve matches." I could see in my mind the matches standing in a row where I'd planted them. They seemed to be translating this to the big lady with the yellow hair and tears came into her eyes. She said something in her language and the important man said to me, "Would you like to come to the city with us?"

I didn't know what to say. I felt I'd rather stay with the bouncing boats and be useful, but everybody seemed to think it was a good thing for me to go to the city. I thought: *perhaps it will*

be nice if they send me there some day, so I made the
sign of agreeing, bending my head and neck sideways. The jute lady didn't seem to know whether
I was saying yes or no, but when they explained
that I'd agreed she patted me on the head and
seemed to forget about me.

After a lot more talk they started moving back
into the boat and somebody said to me, "Hurry
up!" I asked if they were going to the city in the
boat and they laughed. I got in and we drove across
the water to the airplane. The lady and the important man were helped onto the plane and then
the man who was helping them held out his hand
to me. I didn't know whether he was saying hullo
or goodbye. What he said was "Come on!"

They wanted me to go in the airplane! And
only a few days ago I hadn't really believed that
airplanes had people in them at all.

I climbed in. I'd thought an airplane must
feel free like a bird, but here I was shut up in a
very small room with four other people. They put
me in a seat and tied me down with a strap. I
was going to struggle to get free but I saw all
the others were being treated the same way, so I
sat there unhappily. The engines started roaring
and the noise went right through me. We sailed
forward across the water and showers of spray rose
up on both sides. Then the water fell away and
my stomach with all the good food in it seemed

to fall too. We were flying. Through the glass I could see the water racing along below on one side and the palm trees of the coast doing the same the other side. Soon the water was just a piece of wrinkled cloth far below, and the islands were green-brown stains on it.

We circled in the air above a small greenish blob and the man who worked the airplane turned his face to me, pointed downward and shouted something. It was too noisy to make out what he was saying, but the important gentleman put his mouth near my ear and said, "Kukuri Mukuri Char." I couldn't believe that the shapeless blob down there, surrounded by gray-brown water, was the island where I'd been born, and spent eleven years of my life, and lived alone on roots and water, and left my twelve matches standing in a row stuck into the earth. I'd expected the land to look some-how more interesting when you were up above it like a bird, but it just looked flatter.

The sea, though, looked huge and endless. I hadn't known there was so much of it though I'd lived by it all my life. But we turned away from the sea and flew high over the land. I supposed the shining strips were rivers, but it was some time before I understood that the tiny specks like grains of rice, trailing V-shaped streaks behind them, were boats.

The rivers below us became narrower and the

air became hazier, and I realized that the clusters of little boxes down there must be houses. I couldn't understand how there could be so many close together. I hadn't seen a town, so it made no sense to me from the air.

We started coming down then. I remembered that this airplane had come down like a duck on the water and I was a bit alarmed when we seemed to be coming down on the land this time. The earth seemed to tilt over, paddy fields, grass, huge buildings were rushing toward us. I knew my last moment had come and I covered my eyes. There was a jolt, though not as strong as the bouncing boat had given me. I opened my eyes. The earth was still rushing past. I shut them again. Then the noise of the engines grew quieter, and when I opened my eyes again things were only moving slowly.

But what things! I could see that the huge buildings were *baris* for airplanes, for there they were sitting inside them. We passed so close to a vast shining thing, towering over us, that I couldn't make it out as a monstrous airplane standing on its wheels until we'd got some distance away from it again. In one corner there was a group of dark green machines like the first one that had come down on the island. I recognized them like friends. What puzzled me were the square box-shaped things scurrying across the great open spaces with no wings at all.

Our airplane rolled across the flat field and came to a stop near the buildings. The engines stopped and I was glad for the quietness. They opened the doors and we got out. I breathed the air. You don't get very good air in airplanes, but it didn't seem much better outside.

The sun was setting. I was glad to see that it looked more or less like the sun I was used to, though there was a brownish mist that covered its red face. I wondered what we would do now that we had reached the city. Would we sleep in the great *baris* with the airplanes?

There was talk between the people I had travelled with and some others like them who had been standing on the ground. While I waited for it to stop I noticed that our airplane had grown wheels this time to come down on the land, though I was sure I hadn't seen them before. Then we got into another machine. Its noise wasn't very loud but it was soon moving forward pretty fast. I was surprised when it didn't climb into the sky or tilt or bounce or dip or sway. Of course now I know it was a motorcar, but I was too confused to ask about it then.

Everything was so strange. The sun had set. On the islands, when the sun sets, we have only the distant moon and the stars, and the cooking fires of the *baris* and an oil lamp or two. Here there were stars captured on top of rows of tall poles and machines rushing at us with pairs of glaring eyes or rushing ahead with glowing red sparks behind them. Soon there were buildings on each side of us, spilling light out of big square windows. At a place where we stopped there was a round red light that changed to yellow and then to green, and up against the sky were great letters written in lights.

In and out of these flashing, gleaming lights moved shapes; some meant something to me and some meant nothing at all: hundreds of men, no different from our island men, and machines on four wheels, three wheels, or two wheels; cows and oxcarts; great metal boxes packed with people, and with almost as many people clinging to the outside of them. Our motorcar stopped at a great gate across the road and there was a rumbling and a roaring of a different kind of engine, and another great machine went past in front of us, rolling with iron wheels on iron beams. It seemed never-ending, as long as our island, and it too was packed with people inside, and there were even some on top.

I understood nothing of all this, but I had to ask one question and there was only the important gentleman to ask.

"Where are all these people going?" I asked. But he only laughed and said he wished he knew.

I can't tell you about everything that happened that night, it was too strange to remember it all. I remember stopping by a great wall of lighted windows towering to the sky. The door was opened by a tall man dressed in rich clothes who I thought must be the Raja of the city. We walked into a palace of glass where light and music came from nowhere. More men in fine clothes took the bags from the lady and the important gentleman, and a man behind a low wall gave them golden keys. We walked past big rooms. In one of them people were sitting on chairs at tables with white cloths on them, pushing food into their mouths with silver tools to the sound of music. In another, men were sitting sadly on high stools, and they only had something to drink and a few nuts.

But the room we were taken to was no larger than our hut on the island. It was full of people and two heavy doors slid shut in front of our faces. I thought: *it's a prison after all,* and I wanted to cry out, but I had this feeling of flying in my stomach. The doors opened again and the glass palace had vanished. There was only a long tunnel like the ones on the ship, but with soft cloth under our feet.

We came to a door, which someone opened

with the golden key, went into a room—Oh, I can't describe it any more. I think it was then that I sat down on the floor and cried for the strangeness of it all.

They asked me if I was hungry and I said, "No, I have eaten today." But they brought me food and I was surprised to find it was real rice and meat. They put me into a washing machine again—I mean a place full of pipes and white troughs—where I washed myself. And after that I must have slept.

Tape 7:
PROBLEM OF EDUCATIONAL DROPOUTS

The place where I spent my first night in the city was Hell.

No, that's not the word for it. Ho something. Hotel. Anyway I'm glad I didn't stay there very long. After that they put me in a school.

Have you been to a school? You have? Then I won't bother to tell you all about mine. Anyhow most of it was rather dull, after the first bit.

I was taken in a car and put into a huge room full of seats. There was just one boy there, about my age. We sat in silence for quite a long time until at last I said, "My name's Apu."

"My name's Mia," he said.

"I come from the islands," I said.

"I come from the country," he said.

"Are you going to this school?" I asked him.

"I think so," he replied.

A man with a white beard came in—afterward I knew he was a teacher—carrying some papers. He asked me if I had a pencil. Of course I'd seen pencils before but I'd never owned one. He found me a pencil and told us we had to do a test. He gave us each two papers, one plain and one covered with writing. Then he went to a desk and began writing on some papers of his own.

I sat and looked at the sharp black point of my pencil, its sliced wood that had a pleasant smell and its shiny paint. I noticed that Mia was covering his paper with writing and I bent over to admire the way he was making patterns of ink on the white paper, loops and squiggles hanging downward from the lines. The teacher looked up and said sharply, "No copying!" As if I could possibly have copied all those letters!

Mia finished writing, then looked at my empty page.

"Can't you do it?" he whispered. I shook my head. I didn't even have any idea what I was supposed to do.

"I'll do it for you if you'll be my friend," he

whispered. I thought this was pretty good—to have a friend *and* to have my work done for me. So he did it all over again in pencil on my paper. Then the teacher collected the papers and we were allowed to go.

After more waiting about we were taken to another room where there was a very busy man surrounded by people. He had papers in his hands—I suppose they were the ones Mia had written—and he said sternly to me, "Did you copy this?" For some reason Mia looked rather frightened, but I just thought it was a silly question to ask me, when I couldn't even write, so I said firmly "No," and he seemed to be satisfied.

The man—afterward they told me he was the headmaster—asked Mia what school he had been to before, and he gave the name of some village. Then he asked me the same question, but before I could answer a black thing on his desk began to make a loud noise. He wrenched off a part of it and started shouting rather angrily at it. This went on for quite a long time and when he finished he didn't ask me the question again but just said, "You'll both read in class six."

This sounded all right. Class six turned out to be a room full of about seventy boys. But it was a great disappointment to me to find that I couldn't read, although the headmaster had said

71

that I would. Well, I'd never expected to fly, but I did fly, and I thought it might be the same with reading. For days I tried to read but reading never came. I suppose I decided that school wasn't much use, and made up my mind to go back to the islands.

The teachers didn't notice me particularly. If it was my turn to read I'd just repeat the last sentence somebody had spoken and the teacher would say crossly, "We've done that!" and move on to the next boy. If it was writing, either Mia would do it for me or I wouldn't do it at all. The teacher would be quite glad to have one less paper to mark.

I did learn some words though, and they helped me to understand the things I'd seen. Words like "helicopter" and "tin opener," "airport" and "bathroom," "amphibian" and "bus." I got these words mostly from the boys, not the teachers. I once tried to describe the strange experience I'd had in the great building floating on the sea with the white humming tunnels and the roomful of airplanes that went up through the ceiling. Most of the boys just didn't believe me, but there was one who read quite a lot of magazines and he said the word "aircraft carrier." After that the whole thing felt a little less extraordinary; people believed me and I didn't even dream about it so much. And when I learnt that the word "cyclone" meant trees blowing down and the water being heaped up in a great wave and people drowning and houses being carried away, I knew it wasn't only something that had happened to me. They hadn't had the cyclone in the city but everyone was talking about it. I was quite popular with the other boys because I'd been in it, so I didn't mind school, apart from the lessons.

Oh, and we played games.

I slept in a bed in a dormitory and ate three meals a day. Some of the boys said the food wasn't very good, and they didn't even understand when I said it was better than nothing. They'd never tried nothing.

I enjoyed the games. One was throwing balls at a boy standing by himself. He had a club to defend himself with and he was called a batsman. Another game was throwing bits of brick at men called policemen. They had round shields to protect themselves and were more difficult to hit. I only saw the big boys playing this.

Of course the actual lessons usually meant nothing to me. I would sit there quite comfortably, thinking of the next meal, while the voices of the teachers and of clever boys like Mia droned on. But one day I was surprised to find that I seemed to be understanding what they were talking about.

73

There was a big paper hanging on the wall and the more I looked at it the more it reminded me of the day I'd flown in the airplane from the islands, though even then I couldn't understand how flying through the air could be like looking at a paper on the wall. On the paper were patches of blue, and green-brown splodges. I suddenly blurted out, "It looks like islands!" and all the class laughed and cheered, because I'd hardly ever opened my mouth in class before.

The teacher was quite pleased with me and said yes they *were* islands. Then I thought: *they're going to laugh at me anyhow, I might as well ask a really silly question.*

I said, "Which one is Kukuri Mukuri Char?" As I expected, the boys all laughed. I think it was just the name that sounded funny to them. (Oh, you think it sounds funny too?) But the teacher rapped on his desk for silence, went to the map on the wall and—after quite a bit of searching—pointed to a tiny tiny dot. Then—I shall always be fond of that teacher—he said to the rest of the class, "There! Apu knows a bit of geography nobody else knows."

After all the other boys had gone at the end of the lesson I stood in front of the map and stared at the streaks of rivers and the splodges of big islands and the blue sea and the tiny dot near the bottom that was Kukuri Mukuri Char. I was proud that the teacher had said I knew geography. But all I wanted was to get back home.

And it was about that time that all the boys were talking about some men who had gone to the moon. I was pretty sure it was only teasing to begin with, but when one of the teachers mentioned it I supposed it must be true. I thought: *if men can get to the moon, I can get back to my island somehow.* Of course the moon was up there in the sky, everybody could see it, and my island was out of sight somewhere. But I didn't think it could be farther than the moon.

They even gave me money to spend at the school. I don't know where it came from and I didn't even think of asking; it didn't seem important because I had very little idea of what to do with it except buy sticky sweets from a barrow outside the school. For weeks I never went far beyond the main gates, but one day Mia and I wandered out and went toward the market.

I was so sorry for some of the people in the streets. They looked thinner and hungrier than anyone I'd seen in the islands, and there were so many beggars who were blind or old or twisted or without arms or legs. I gave a little coin to a blind old man with a beard and he praised God. A boy of about my age saw me giving money and came up to me and asked for some. I gave him a small coin too, and he said it wasn't enough and that he was starving. I was very sorry for him, so I repeated what Abdurrahman and the man on the ship had told me: "The airplanes and boats and soldiers are there to help you."

He laughed in my face as if it was the most foolish saying he'd ever heard. I was tired of being laughed at by people who knew better than me, and he was only a poor ignorant boy like myself.

"What are you laughing at?" I said. "I have seen the airplanes and the boats bringing food and clothes and blankets to the poor people."

He said he'd heard about the things arriving in airplanes. He'd gone to the airport at night and tried to get some. He'd climbed over some buildings and down a pillar but the soldiers had seen him and chased him away. "Help me?" he scoffed. "They wouldn't even let me help myself!"

"You should go to the islands," I said.

"If they are giving things away on the islands why did you leave them?" he asked me.

I told him they'd brought me here on an airplane and I didn't know how to get back.

"Come to the docks tonight," he said. "We'll find a ship and go down together."

Mia had been fidgeting all through this conversation and wanting to go on. I asked him if he'd come with me to the islands, as he was my friend, but he said they weren't his islands and he intended to stay at school. I suppose it was all right for him; he was doing well at school and he was much cleverer than me. So I arranged to meet the beggar boy alone that evening. He told me his name was Khoka.

I don't know whether they ever missed me at that school. Oh, they were always calling out lists of names while the teacher made marks in a book. For a long time I thought a lesson meant learning the names of the seventy boys in the class. But I asked Mia and some other boys to answer for me after I'd gone, so perhaps they never noticed I wasn't there.

That evening I put on the good clothes I'd been given in the boat, stepped out into the street and walked toward the market. I met Khoka and he said, "Come on, let's take a rickshaw!" I chose a beautiful new-looking one with a blue roof covered with white patterns, stiff red plastic flowers sprouting from its tubes, spinning plastic propellers like an airplane's on its handles and a picture of a man singing to a lady on the back. I said to the rickshaw man, "You must be rich to own such a beautiful rickshaw." He said he didn't own it, he only pedaled it all day and had to give most of the money to the owner, but he was quite proud that it was so new and beautiful. I asked him if he'd let me pedal it. He seemed pleased and got in the back with Khoka while I sat on the seat, put my feet on the pedals and held the handlebars. Going straight was quite easy, though turning corners was more difficult than it looked, and I soon found it was hard work pedaling all the time and I felt sorrier than ever for the poor men who had to keep going all day.

Khoka told me the way and the rickshaw man told me how to take care in the traffic, stopping at the red lights and ringing my bell at people in the way. I was afraid of the motorcars at first, but as we went toward the center of the Old Town the cars became swamped in the never-ending stream of hundreds and thousands of rickshaws flowing through the narrow streets.

We got to a place where I could see water and boats through gaps between the buildings, and Khoka told me to stop. We got down and the rickshaw man asked for money. When I gave him a piece of paper money he said it wasn't enough, so I gave him a silvery coin as well. He went on demanding more but Khoka started calling him names and pointing out that I'd done all the work anyhow. He took the money and went off laughing and telling the other rickshaw men how he made me pay for pedaling his rickshaw.

I didn't know there were so many people in the world as I saw along the riverside: crowds walking all over the streets, people sitting patiently on bundles, people sleeping on the pavement surrounded by their cooking pots and bunches of bananas. There were shops selling everything from cooking stoves to schoolbooks, though not many people seemed to be buying.

On the river there were almost as many boats as there were people in the streets: huge boats with great wheels on each side; dozens like the one on which I met the pig eaters; big country boats with tall sterns and sharp beaks ghosting down the river under square sails, the lights from the far shore shining through their thin cloth; all over the water small wooden boats coming and going, their boatmen paddling, pulling oars, pushing oars or sculling over the stern with big flat oars.

"Where are all these people going?" I asked Khoka, then remembered I'd asked the question before. Khoka didn't know the answer either. He just said we had to find a boat going to the islands.

We walked along the riverside to a quiet place and Khoka spoke to a man in a small boat. He whispered for quite a long time. I didn't hear everything he said, but the boatman seemed to be repeating, "Yes, yes, to Tazumuddin." The name meant nothing to me. Khoka showed the boatman some money—I was surprised he had so much—then he got into the boat and told me to get in too.

The boatman—he was a very old man—paddled the leaky boat out into the darkness with a broken paddle.

"Are we going to the islands in this?" I asked Khoka. Boats are something I do know about, and I didn't think much of this one. Khoka said no, and told me to keep quiet and follow him quickly when he got out of the boat. I don't know why I felt quite happy to take his word for everything. Perhaps it was because he seemed to be quite certain where he was going.

We drifted down in the dark to a long, low shape that seemed to be anchored in the river. It was different from all the other vessels, something like the square boats the soldiers used but very much bigger. On its long deck I could see a mountain of cargo in great sacks.

Khoka told me to lie in the bottom of the boat. It was difficult to do without getting soaked in bilge water. I did my best to keep my good clothes dry. Our boat bumped clumsily against the iron side of the other vessel. Someone on board swore at us and the old boatman replied feebly. We scraped all the way down the side of the ship, with the watchkeeper cursing us all the time. Khoka kept clutching me so I couldn't move. Then as we drifted into the shadow under the great square bows he whispered, "Come on!" He jumped up, caught the rail, and climbed under it onto the ship. I followed him. Immediately we made a dive for the mountain of sacks and tucked ourselves under the big cloth that covered them. The little boat drifted away in the darkness without a farewell.

I don't know how long we lay there in silence, hearing only the river trickling past and the coughing and spitting of the watchkeeper. I went to sleep and I think Khoka did too. What woke me was the ringing of bells, the sound of a great engine beating through the iron deck and the clank of the anchor chain as it was hauled in. Then we could hear the water rushing past and we knew we were on the move.

Under cover of all these noises we thought it was safe to talk in low voices.

"Are you sure this will take us to Kukuri Mukuri?" was the first thing I asked.

"Most of the way, anyhow," Khoka said. I asked him how he knew and he said his employers had found out.

"I thought you were a beggar," I said.

"You don't think I beg all by myself, do you?" he said. "I'm not as poor as all that."

I said I didn't understand, so as we chugged through the night he told me about the beggars' gang that employed him. He explained that though he had to give his employer a lot of the money he got by begging it was better than being all alone in the world. The gang arranged the best places for begging, like the post offices and the red lights where the cars had to stop, and they made sure the places didn't get too crowded. It was the same when he got money for looking after parked cars. If people didn't pay for a car watchman the gang made sure that a bit of car was missing when the owner came back. The gang bosses got quite a lot of money in this way, but since the cyclone they had heard of fabulous riches being given away in the islands, so they were sending people down there to see what they could get. But it helped to go down with somebody who belonged to the islands. He asked me if I'd tell people he was one of my family, in case we were asked questions.

Well, I liked Khoka and I didn't mind helping him, especially as he was helping me get home. But I didn't feel the same about helping a gang.

"Will you go back to the gang?" I asked.

"I'll have to," he said. "Otherwise they'll come after me."

"Why don't you just stay down in the islands with me?" I asked him. "It's much better than the city. Or it used to be." It suddenly occurred to me that I'd been imagining going back to the life I knew in the islands before the cyclone.

"They'll come after me," he repeated. "They know where I'm going, otherwise they couldn't have told me how to get there. Anyhow the gang are the only friends I've got."

"What about your family?" I asked.

"I don't know anything about my family," he said. According to the gang, Khoka had been given to a beggar woman to carry about when he was a tiny baby. As soon as he could walk he learnt to beg for himself. Now of course he was getting too big for it. People were only sorry for women with babies or little children, or the very old or blind or crippled. He didn't want to have to cut his hand off to make people sorry for him.

I said I was glad I lived in the islands, even with cyclones, if the city was like that. I told him all the things that had happened to me.

"You mean we may have to live on river water and radishes!" he exclaimed when I'd finished. I said I'd rather do that than be a beggar. We were pretty silent after that, but anyhow we couldn't turn back now. We peeped out from under the cover and all we could see was a great searchlight shining into the darkness ahead, its beam full of nightmoths, as the iron ship churned through the empty river. There was nothing to do but settle down to sleep on the rather hard sacks.

Tape 8:
RELIEF GOODS
SHIPPED TO
ISLANDS

When I woke up again there was daylight showing under the edges of the cover. The engines were still drumming away and we were still moving through the water. I woke Khoka and asked him how we were going to get off the ship in daylight without being seen. I could see him rubbing his eyes and blinking, and he had to say he'd never thought of that. They'd told him that he'd reach the islands before daylight, but it must have been further than they thought.

"Never mind," he said. "If they find us they can't kill us, and we'll have got there anyhow." I was glad again to have him as a traveling companion. He wasn't the worrying sort.

We arranged a peephole in the cover and watched the coast gliding past in the gray dawn light. I could see the cyclone had been there. There were dead branchy trees lying on their sides and battered palms leaning over toward the south. Khoka wasn't much interested, it wasn't his coast, but every now and then I nudged him and made him look at things. There was a big ship lying among paddy fields, far away from the water's edge. Further on there was a gap in the sea wall high above the water level and in it sat, high and dry, a large launch. There were *bari* mounds swept bare of houses, and in other places shacks of palm leaves with people squatting in them. Here and there were solitary figures, sometimes children, standing on the empty shore looking out toward us. I thought of how I'd stood alone on the shore, but I couldn't make this ship stop to help.

I suddenly felt cold and empty and afraid. Was I going back to live on roots again? You can live like that if you don't know any better, but it's different going back to it after three meals a day.

The figure of a sailor passed right in front of my peephole. I froze and kept still. Another passed and another. They seemed to be busy with something in the front of the ship. The engines

85

slowed down, the rushing of the water alongside us grew less, and there was a sudden tremendous rattling and clanking that shook the whole ship as if it was falling to pieces. I almost jumped out of my hiding place, but by peering round the side of my peephole I could see that the noise was made by the anchor chain running out. The bells clanged and the engine stopped. I knew we must have arrived.

I looked out at the shore again. Broken palm trees, muddy banks. It might have been anywhere, though there was a tent near the shore, and some soldiers. What next? We lay under the heavy cloth and I felt hungry again.

"I'm hungry," I whispered to Khoka.

"There's food all around us," he said. He brought out a little knife and cut a hole in the bag we were lying on. Some white flour spilled out and we put some in our mouths and swallowed it. It was not very interesting food but it was better than nothing.

There was a bumping against the side of the ship and the sound of a lot of voices talking the way we talk in the islands. I peeped out and saw a country boat. The people in it were holding on to the side of the ship and asking for food. I heard the words: "We are hungry. Our village is destroyed and we have no food."

A sailor on the ship replied roughly, "Shove off! This food has to go on to the relief center. You can line up there and take your turn."

"Just one sack!" begged the man in the boat.

"I know you," said the sailor. "You're a lot of pirates." I wondered whether it was Abdurrahman and his gang or just a boatload of starving villagers. The sailor didn't seem to care.

It was funny. Here was a mountain of food for the islanders. Here were we, eating it in secret and feeling like thieves. There was a boatload of people and they weren't getting anything.

I could see more country boats paddling out from the shore and clustering around the ship. I had an idea and began wriggling out of my good clothes underneath the tarpaulin. I did my trousers and jacket up in a bundle and wrapped my red shirt round me like a loin cloth. Now I looked like Khoka and like any of the islanders on the boats.

I whispered to Khoka, "Come on! To the boats!" He looked a bit surprised that I was telling him what to do, but then he nodded. I just crawled out on to the deck and walked toward the rail, followed by Khoka.

The sailor saw us and shouted, "Hey! You two! Get back into the boat!" He thought we'd just climbed aboard. All I wanted was to get into one of the boats so I said, "All right, I'm going," and moved to the side. But the sailor rushed at me and snatched my bundle of clothes.

"Thief!" he shouted. "Where did you get that from?"

"It's mine," I protested.

He looked at the good trousers, jacket and shoes. "You've stolen it from the cabins," he said. Then he turned to another sailor and said, "Here, grab these two. They've been thieving. We'll hand them over to the police."

We didn't wait to argue but jumped over the rail, onto the nearest boat, and then climbed across several boats until we came to one on the outside of the cluster. The sailors didn't bother to follow.

The men in this boat weren't too pleased to see us either. They asked us who we were and where we'd come from.

"I'm from Kukuri Mukuri," I said. "Where's this?" They said it was Tazumuddin.

"Can we get food and clothes here?" Khoka asked.

"There's plenty," said the man. "But you can't get it because it's a relief center." I asked him what he meant.

"The stuff's coming in all the time. They are landing it by shiploads and dropping it from the skies, but you get nothing unless you belong here."

88

"How do they know if you belong?" Khoka asked.

"You have to have your name on the paper," the man said.

"And if you don't?" I asked.

"You have to go back to your own village and wait," said the boatman. "That's what the sailor's just told us to do. But it's a long way and the food may take a long time coming."

"What about the rubber boats and the helicopter?" I asked.

"They come and they go. If God wills they'll find us," he said. There didn't seem to be any use in hanging round there, so they pushed off and began rowing away. They said their village was on the way to Kukuri Mukuri and they didn't mind giving us a lift in that direction.

They were simple village people and they certainly had no food on board their boat. The boat itself was leaky and battered and must have gone through the cyclone somewhere, and the men were so weak that I had to help them row part of the way. Even Khoka had a go on the big steering oar but he found it was more difficult than it looked and we nearly lost him overboard.

After a long hard row we turned up a river mouth, then up a small creek that led into the river, and at last arrived at a little village miles from anywhere. The cyclone had been there all right. The huts were patched up from bits and pieces. Outside them were women and children, sitting around cooking pots.

"You have some food then," Khoka said.

"Praise God we have cooking pots and fire, and water for cooking," said our host. "And if you can eat the bark of trees you are welcome to share our food."

It was not quite as bad as it sounded, though it was bad enough. It was a juicy kind of green stem they were boiling in water. It made a very thin vegetable soup that you could drink, and you could chew the woody bits and pretend you were eating. It was kind of them to give it to Khoka and me who were only strangers, and I felt bad, being another hungry mouth in this hungry land. At least I was feeling that I was nearer home, but Khoka was very gloomy.

"Is this your land where free food falls from the heavens?" he grumbled. "I'd be better off minding cars in the city. Even the cows there don't eat trees."

That afternoon a country boat came up the creek and stopped at the village. We could see it was loaded with goods and guarded by men like soldiers. A man in shirt and trousers landed, holding a paper. He called for the head man of the village and as we all gathered round he read out a list of all the families. The head man checked the list with him and got all the people lined up. This took a long time. Then men were chosen to carry goods from the boat and they started to dole out rice and flour.

Of course Khoka and I weren't on the list. Khoka tried more than once to sneak into one of the lines but the families got angry and drove him out. They'd shared with us their wretched bits of tree bark, but somehow it was different giving away this free food.

The man with the shirt and trousers looked at Khoka and me standing apart and asked me where I came from. I said I'd come from Kukuri Mukuri Char. He asked me how. So I started to tell him: First of all I floated away on a tree but it came back again, or at least I think it did. Then the helicopter came but it didn't take me. Then the soldiers landed and took me to the ship and I climbed down the chain and I joined the pirates and they took me back again. So there I was where I'd started from—or I think I was. Then the rubber boats came and took me to the launch and the airplane took me to the city and I came back on the ship with the sacks of flour. I'm hungry—

He stopped me and said that was enough. I don't think he believed a word of it. He said I'd have to go back to my own village if I wanted free food, and I mustn't take food from other people. Then Khoka started telling him how he'd never had any father or mother and hadn't eaten for a week, and he spoke so sadly that he made me cry, though I knew it wasn't all true. But I think he did it too well, and the man just said, "Go away, beggar boy!"

It seemed we had to move on, but there weren't any speedboats or airplanes around this time. The only thing we could do was ask the gentleman if he'd take us away in his boat. He wasn't very keen to do it but at last he let us get on board. He told the guards to keep an eye on us to see we didn't take any of the food. Khoka pretended to be angry, and said, "Do you think we are thieves?" Of course the man just said yes.

The boat took us slowly down the creek and then further and further up the river. This wasn't what I wanted. I knew we could only get to Kukuri Mukuri by water and it was no use going inland.

We came to a big village where there were brick houses and tin sheds, and they landed and took us to the police station. I was sure I was going to be asked questions again, and this time I felt so tired of it all that I said to Khoka, "You do the talking. But don't try too hard."

Khoka was clever this time. This was how he answered the questions:

"What's your name?"

"Khoka. I remember my name is Khoka."

"Where is your village?"

"I don't know. I don't remember."

"Where is your family?"

"I don't remember my family. The water came . . ."

Then he cried. I suppose the words he said were more or less true, anyway they made people sorry for him. When they asked me questions I said the same sort of thing, and it was more true when I said it but they didn't seem to believe it as much. They didn't seem to know what to do with us, but luckily the policemen were having their meal and when they'd finished we had what was left over. It was good rice and vegetables and we felt better. We ate it in the kitchen of the police station and when we'd finished Khoka said, "Come on!"

"They haven't said we can go," I said. But he wouldn't wait. I don't think he liked policemen much, in spite of the good meal they'd given us. He took me by the arm, we slipped out the back way and ran off.

In between the houses there was a road full of potholes and on it stood a very old bus. It was loaded with sacks inside and baskets and bundles on top.

Khoka said, "Let's get on." I'd never been

on a bus and I thought it might be interesting so I said, "All right. Shall we ask the driver?" Khoka told me not to be a fool but to get ready to climb up the ladder at the back on to the top.

A guard with a stick was standing behind the bus and the driver was just getting in at the front. I could see that if we tried to get on while it was standing still or moving away the guard would stop us, and I wondered what Khoka would do.

He did nothing until the driver got in and started up the engine, and the bus started to move slowly away. Then I thought he'd gone crazy and tried to kill himself. He seemed to throw himself under the front wheel, and he screamed horridly. The bus stopped with a jolt, the guard ran round to the front, Khoka crawled quickly to the back and went up the ladder like lightning. I followed him. While the guard and the driver were peering under the front, looking for the body, we were hiding among the bundles on top.

My heart was pounding. "Never do that again!" I whispered fiercely. The village people were clustering round the front of the bus, shouting angrily at the bus driver and blaming him for the accident. He kept shouting back, "Look underneath! Look underneath! There's nobody there!" They didn't think of looking on top, so at last the bus was allowed to drive off.

I think that the trip on the top of the bus was the worst of all my travels. The bouncing boats had been fun, but the top of a bouncing bus isn't. We didn't go very fast, but there were holes all over the road which the bus kept falling into, and it was only the ropes with which the bundles were tied on that stopped us from being bounced off. One bundle had very sharp edges that kept sticking into us, and Khoka took out his little knife and cut it open to see what was in it.

"Books!" he exclaimed in disgust. They were like the things the teachers wrote our names in at school. "What's the use of books?" Khoka went on. "They don't feed you or keep you warm and they're not even comfortable to lie on. I haven't come all this way to get books."

After a time we just sat up on top of the bus. We knew the driver couldn't see us and we waved at the villagers who stood hopefully at the roadside and watched our load of goods go past.

"Where do you think we're going?" I asked Khoka.

"Away from those policemen anyway," he said. But soon we were coming into a township where there seemed to be just as many policemen and soldiers, and there were tents full of sacks and lines of people waiting for food.

Khoka said he didn't think much of the look

of this place either. We decided to wait till the bus slowed down and then jump off and run for it. A policeman, or a soldier, saw us doing it and blew a whistle at us. We ran out of the village onto a narrow, dusty track between paddy. Nobody seemed to be following us so we slowed down to a walk. I pulled some ears of rice as we went and looked at them closely. The leaves were yellow and dying and the grains were not very big and looked mouldy. It was rice, but not very good rice. I thought of the three meals a day that used to appear at school and wondered why I'd come back to this poor land.

We caught up with a wooden cart pulled by a pair of water buffaloes. On it was one full sack, some blankets and one old man. Khoka jumped up on the back of the cart. I thought it would be more polite to ask the driver for a lift first, but I did the same. We rode in silence for a while except for the loud creaking of the wheels. When the old man still took no notice of us we couldn't help giggling and whispering.

At last, without turning his head, the old man spoke a greeting. I answered and then said, "Where are we?"

"I may be blind," said the old man, "but I know you're sitting on the back of my cart."

"Blind?" Khoka exclaimed. "How do you

know where you're going if you're blind?"

"Is the sun to the right of us?" the old man asked. I said it was. "Then we're going south," he said. "My buffaloes know the road."

"Why don't you stay at home if you're blind?" I asked.

"You get no food if you stay at home and wait for it," he answered. I said I thought people were *supposed* to stay at home and wait for it.

"When I was young," the old man began. I could hear Khoka groan at these words—he hated history—but luckily the groaning of the cart wheels drowned his rudeness. "When I was young we used to sow the seed in the ground and water it and plant it out and water it again and wait for the harvest." (Khoka chanted a mocking tune to the groaning of the wheels.) "Then when it was ripe," the old man continued, "we would cut it and thresh it and mill it and boil it and eat it. And if the salt water spoiled it or the pests destroyed it or there was no water to make it grow, then we starved. But now, some say they will give us food in the towns, and some say they will bring it to us in the villages. They say the food is coming in boats and in buses. And some say that food even drops from the skies—but I shall only believe that when I see it, and I'm stone blind." He laughed a feeble laugh. I began to tell him about the helicopters and airplanes, but all he said was, "Ah, you're young"—as if that made any difference to airplanes!

I asked him if he knew where Kukuri Mukuri was.

"When I had my sight," he replied, "I used to look over the water from my village to an island which they said was Kukuri Mukuri Char. But I never went there."

Khoka at last pricked up his ears. "So we're nearly there," he said. "About time too. We've come a long way to find one sack of flour on a cart." He looked at the sack.

A shocking idea came to me. "You're not thinking of stealing it, are you?" I whispered.

Now Khoka was shocked. "You don't think I'd steal food from a blind old man, do you?" he exclaimed. "What do you think I am?"

I was beginning to wonder, now that I'd heard we were at last getting near home. Khoka seemed to be so sure that when he got to Kukuri Mukuri he would find what he was looking for. But what was it? And I was beginning to doubt if we'd find anything at all.

The buffaloes plodded along the track and the sun sank down the western sky. Khoka kept fidgeting impatiently, and standing up in the cart to look ahead. But there was nothing to see except tattered trees, until at last we came to the remains of a village. The *baris* were just odds and ends of matting and corrugated iron propped against treetrunks, but through one group of trees we could see new white buildings.

The buffaloes stopped of their own accord. "We have arrived," said the old man. He began to call the names of his family, but there was no reply. "We are at the village, aren't we?" he asked. "They should be waiting for me."

I said all the people seemed to be over by the new white buildings. At that the old man appeared quite bewildered. "New white buildings? What are you talking about? There are no new white buildings in the village. You are not mocking a poor old man, are you?"

He looked so puzzled and helpless, sitting there in the front of the cart, that I felt very sorry for him. I told him to stay there while Khoka and I went to find out what was happening.

We ran across to the clump of trees. I was not surprised to find a row of tents the other side. There was a small crowd of villagers outside them, and when I asked if anyone owned a blind grandfather and two buffaloes a woman walked off to see about it.

Khoka pushed his way to the front of the crowd and I followed. When we got near the tents

Khoka nudged me and gasped, "Look at all that stuff!"

I looked. There were beautiful shining chairs and tables, dozens and dozens of bottles, silvery tools of all sorts and stacks of unopened crates. But it was all guarded by three strange creatures, tall, with white faces, white things on their heads, long white dresses, white stockings and even white shoes, though these were a little muddy and dusty.

The villagers were hanging back, looking at them suspiciously. I suppose it was because Khoka was the only town boy, and was used to strange sights, that he was able to go up to the strange creatures and address them, while I followed one step behind.

"Is that stuff for us?" Khoka asked boldly.

The three tall, white women—I decided they must be women—turned to each other as if they hadn't understood the question. Then they grabbed us! They were strong, but I could have wriggled out of their grasp if I hadn't seen that Khoka wasn't struggling. They led us into the tent—I suppose that was what Khoka wanted.

But he got more than he bargained for. I watched while he was looked at, poked, listened to, pricked, bled, scratched on the arm and pumped full of stuff from a needle. I couldn't help grinning at him as he kept his lips tightly shut—

100

except when they made him open his mouth and stuck some cotton on a stick down his throat. At one moment his eyes were glaring furiously at me as I laughed at him, then defiantly at the women, daring them to do their worst with him. But mostly his eyes were on all the valuable things in the tent and I could see he was wondering how much he could get away with.

Then it was his turn to laugh, as they did all the same things to me. I tried to tell the women I'd had it all before on the ship, and some of it at school too, but they didn't understand. Anyhow, I thought all this poking and pricking was somehow supposed to make you better, though in my experience you always felt sicker at the end of it.

It wasn't until we'd both been thoroughly gone over that a woman came to the tent who, though she was dressed like the others, was one of our people and spoke our language. After talking with the three white ladies she told us that I was a fine healthy boy but that Khoka needed some medicines. I was going to say that it was because he came from the city that he wasn't very healthy, but he kicked me on the ankle just in time to stop me. Then the nurse explained that the other three nurses had flown six thousand miles to help the people in the islands and had brought all those things with them.

In the end we didn't get much out of the nurses. They gave us a meal. There was some rice, but nothing spicy or tasty, only some grayish powder mixed with it. They said it would make us big and strong, but it didn't taste very strong.

As soon as we'd eaten Khoka started saying, "Let's go!" The sun was very low and I thought it would be better to spend the night in the tents. "The nurses may give us something if we stay," I said.

"I've had enough of what the nurses give," Khoka said. "There were some nice knives and scissors but I'm not fighting those she-dragons for them. I'm wounded already."

So we slipped out of the tent as we had slipped out of the police station, and headed south. It wasn't far to the shore, just beyond the belt of battered trees. There the land ran flat to a low edge, then mudbanks sloped gently into shallow brown water. To the west the big red sun was dipping toward the water. To the south was a long dark smudge with a few feathery treetops sticking out of it.

"The old man said he used to be able to see Kukuri Mukuri from here," said Khoka. "That must be it, mustn't it?"

I said it certainly was an island but I couldn't be sure which.

"Let's go and see," Khoka urged.

I asked him how. He seemed to think I was being difficult. "There must be a boat," he kept saying. I told him most of the boats had been sunk by the cyclone, but Khoka insisted on looking for one. And in the mud of a creek we found one.

It wasn't much of a boat, just a canoe dug out of a log, and it was nearly buried in the mud. I wanted to leave it until next day, but Khoka seemed determined to keep going. He set to work scooping out mud with his two hands and he was soon covered in mud himself. I couldn't leave him to do it alone and before long I was in the same state. Of course it was more difficult than Khoka had expected. I know about boats. The sun went down while we were still mudlarking about in the creek, but a big moon came up and Khoka wouldn't stop working. For a lazy beggar it was amazing how he could work when he wanted to.

We were just able to drag the canoe down to the water between us. We found two pieces of board farther down the beach which would do as paddles, and we pushed the boat out through the shallow water.

I think people sometimes do things which they know are crazy, just because somebody else talks them into it. We couldn't see the island we were heading for, we didn't know if the boat had a leak,

103

we didn't have proper paddles, and I knew it must be farther than Khoka thought it was. But we set off across to the island by moonlight.

When we got clear of the shore the tide caught us. It was swirling in eddies which made it difficult even to keep the boat pointed in the right direction. At least we were moving south—the shore soon faded away northward—but I was afraid that we might get carried out to sea and be lost forever.

I needn't have worried. Before long our short paddles were touching the bottom at every stroke, and then the boat stuck fast on a mudbank.

We tried moving the boat back the way we had come, punting with our paddles against the bottom. I got out of the boat and tried pushing. The water was below my knees. Khoka got out and joined me, but the tide was running out so fast that soon we couldn't even push the empty boat.

I climbed in and sat down, and told Khoka to do the same.

"Where's all the water gone?" he asked. I said the tide had gone out. Khoka had never heard of the tide so I tried to explain it to him.

"It'll come back," I said.

"When?"

"In a few hours."

104

"How do you know?"

"It always does," I said. "At least it always did before the cyclone. I don't know whether everything's changed now."

Khoka wanted to get out and walk.

"Which way?" I asked him. He pointed in the darkness but he didn't sound too sure. I thought the island was in quite a different direction. We'd been pushing and twisting the boat so much that we really had no idea which way we'd come from. The bright moon was nearly overhead and didn't help. I looked up at the stars and tried to remember which was north and which was south. All the island boatmen know these things, of course, and I'd been told but had forgotten. But I did know how fast the tide could come in when it turned, and knew it was one of the rules not to leave a stranded boat when you were far from the shore. I persuaded Khoka to stay. It was chilly out there in the middle of the water and the boat did not make a very comfortable bed, but we both managed to sleep.

I had a dream. I could see Kukuri Mukuri as it used to be, with the thatched bamboo *baris* standing on the mounds and my little cousins playing around them. I was sitting in a rubber boat with wings, trying to paddle toward the island, but instead of a paddle I only had a school book.

I knew that if I could read the book I could use it to paddle myself to the island, but I couldn't and with every stroke I was being carried backward, and behind me there was a great hotel standing in the middle of the sea. I also knew that in the hotel there was someone I'd never seen but who was king of all the beggars and was waiting for me to be carried back to the hotel, where he would turn me into a beggar. Then a voice was saying, "The water's come back! The water's come back!" and I knew I must climb a tree but there weren't any trees to climb, only lampposts with great stars on top . . .

I tried to wake myself up, but the voice was still saying "The water's come back!" Then I knew I was awake and it was Khoka who was saying the words. It took a little time to realize I was on a mudbank in the middle of nowhere and that the tide had returned and the boat was already moving over the mud. One part of the sky was getting light and I knew it must be near dawn.

"Get paddling!" I said to Khoka. "The tide's trying to take us north."

We turned the boat so that the dawn was on our left and paddled as hard as we could. At least it warmed us up after our chilly night, but when it grew light enough to see we sighted land behind us, to the north, and it seemed to be drawing nearer. The tide was taking us backward faster than we could paddle forward. It was just like the dream I'd had.

"It's no use," I said to Khoka. "We'll never get there."

"I'm not going back to those nurses!" said Khoka, gritting his teeth and paddling with all his strength. But we were still drifting back toward a tiny island. It had the thin growth of grass and reeds that makes the difference between a mud-bank and a *char*.

"Come on!" I said. "We'll stop here for a bit." We paddled hard and managed to beach the boat on the bank of the *char* and lift it far enough out of the water to stop it from drifting with the tide. Exhausted, we lay down on the grass.

"What do we do now?" Khoka asked.

"We wait for the tide to go out."

"What's the use?" he demanded. "When it goes out it puts us on a mudbank. When it comes in it takes us back where we started from! I'm glad we don't have anything as stupid as tides in the city."

For some reason I thought of the streams of rickshaws and people flowing through the Old Town, but I didn't feel like arguing. I was quite happy lying back, looking at the empty sky and listening to the water flowing past. The sun was warm and the grass had a good smell.

"This is better than the city," I said. Khoka was quite angry.

"Whatever do you mean?" he exclaimed. "Here we are starving and stuck in the middle of nowhere and you say it's better than the city."

"What do you like doing?" I asked him.

"I'll tell you what I'd like to do," he said. "I once got into the garden of the big hotel in the city and looked through the window. There were men and women wearing expensive clothes sitting at tables. Men in even better clothes were bringing them food. But the people with the best clothes were the musicians who were playing tunes to them. They had jewels all over them. That's where I'd like to be."

I told him I'd stayed in that hotel and didn't think much of it. He got even angrier and said I was telling lies. After that we lay without talking and watched the water flow past.

Khoka said he was thirsty and got up to go down to the water.

"It'll be salty now," I said.

"How do you know?" he asked.

I said, "Try it." He tried it and made a face.

"Useless lot of water!" he said as he came back.

"You've got to take it as it comes," I said.

"No use arguing with it or complaining." He lay down sulkily and said nothing.

The time passed slowly. After a while I stood up and threw a reed stem as far out into the water as I could. It stayed still without drifting.

"Come on!" I said. "Time to catch the tide."

We pushed the boat off again, climbed in, turned its head south and paddled in silence. The winter sun was hot but a little breeze blew from the north and cooled our backs. The sun was ahead of us and its reflections danced on the waves. Looking back at our little *char* I could see that already the current was carrying us in the direction we wanted to go. Beyond the reflections of the sun lay the green strip of shore with ragged trees toward which we were heading.

"Are you sure that's Kukuri Mukuri?" came Khoka's voice from behind me.

"It looks like it," I replied.

"Don't they all look the same?" he asked.

I said, "Yes," and after that we were silent again. I knew I had to keep a look out for different colored patches of water that marked the shallow spots. Every time I altered course to avoid them Khoka asked me what I was doing. When I said I was avoiding mudbanks he accused me of imagining them.

The shapes of things on the shore ahead grew

gradually clearer. I thought I could recognise a certain battered palm and another branchy tree which seemed already to be putting out fresh green leaves. And there was the creek, with boats in it, and there were shapes of buildings among the trees, and people moving between them.

Then I remembered what the island had been like when I left it. Boats? Buildings? People? What would they be doing on my island?

I stopped paddling.

"I'm sorry," I said to Khoka. "We've come to the wrong place."

Tape 9:
RECONSTRUCTION ON KUKURI MUKURI

We drifted slowly toward the shore.

Khoka spoke: "If this isn't Kukuri Mukuri, where is it?"

"I don't know," I said. "I suppose we can ask. Do you think they'll feed us here?"

"They'd better," he said. "I'm starving again."

We paddled toward a landing place. There were two tall soldiers standing there. They waited until we had beached the boat, then one of them said jokingly, "And what's brought you here?"

Questions again. What had brought us there?

I was tired and disappointed and didn't know the right answer. The easiest thing seemed to be to tell the truth. I said: "A rickshaw and a rowing-boat and a cargo boat and two country boats and a bus and a buffalo cart and this canoe. And the tide."

The soldier laughed, but not very pleasantly, and said, "Then you'd better go back."

I felt very weak. "I can't," I said.

"Why not?"

"The tide's going the wrong way."

The soldier spoke with the other soldier in a manner I couldn't follow. They seemed to be talking about the water. Then he turned to me and said, "You'll have to go back on the next tide."

"We're hungry," Khoka said. "Haven't you any food for us?"

"You'll have to ask Mr. Enamel," said the soldier.

I asked who Mr. Enamel was and the soldier said he was the Relief Officer. We left the boat on the beach and they took us to a tent. I was used to finding tents all over the islands and of course the buildings we'd seen were more tents. In the tents were tables and chairs, and the tables were stacked with piles of paper. There was a man sitting on a chair behind one of these piles and I could hardly see his head over the top. He peered over at me through his spectacles. His eyes were neither kind nor unkind, just worried, but my heart sank. I knew it was questions again. They started.

"Name?"

"Apu, or Anisuzzaman."

"Father's name?"

"Bashir."

"Living?"

"No."

"Guardian?"

"Ahmed, son of Kabir. But he's dead too."

"Then he can't be your guardian, can he?" I was surprised that Mr. Enamel could speak a whole sentence, and I didn't know what to say. I preferred the short questions, they were less muddling. A short question came.

"Home?"

Home? Home! Did people have homes? Did I have a home? What was a home? Was it a tent? A *char* in the middle of the water? A mudbank in the middle of the night? A school dormitory? A hotel? A shack made of a broken packing case? A tree floating in a cyclone? My mind spun as I tried to think of the right answer. It was funny, the roof of the tent was spinning too. I felt very strange and the ground was coming up to meet me . . .

I slowly woke up and opened my eyes to see a strange blue light all round me and a white figure standing beside me. Was I in paradise with an angel? No, it was a blue tent with the sunlight shining through the cloth and the figure was a nurse. She asked me how I was, in my own language, then went and fetched a glass from the top of a packing case and offered it to me. It was that watery, powdery milk again, but I was glad to drink it.

I said, "What happened and where am I?" I remember thinking even then it was better to ask questions than answer them. The nurse smiled and told me I had fainted and I was in the hospital tent. Then I asked where Khoka was. She pointed across the tent and I saw Khoka, lying like myself on a mattress on the ground, grinning at me.

When the nurse went out Khoka said, "I fainted too. It seemed the only way to stop them asking questions. At least I lay with my eyes shut while they talked about us. Seems we can't stay on the island unless we're written on the paper and we can't be written on the paper unless we've got permission to stay on the island."

I lay back on my mattress and felt very tired, but Khoka went on: "Don't worry. We're on the hospital list now. So don't be in too much of a hurry to get well."

I looked up at the blue roof. My mind told me I ought to be thinking of moving on, yet I couldn't imagine going any further. In spite of the strange surroundings I had an odd feeling of being at my journey's end—even a feeling of being at home, though there seemed to be no reason for it.

I finished my glass of milk but I was still hungry and I said so to Khoka.

"Why don't you ask for some food then?" Khoka said. "I've had some—real rice and hot chillies. That's what made me want to stay."

The nurse came back and I asked for some food. She said the doctor was on the other side of the island and she didn't know whether I ought to have anything. I told her I'd die of starvation if she didn't feed me, so she began opening a tin. When I saw the gray powder in it I said I needed real food. She knew what I meant and eventually fetched me a plate of rice, vegetables and spices. I shoveled it into my mouth with my fingers and felt that I was myself again.

After the meal I went outside the tent to rinse my hands at a water bucket that stood there, and then sat in the sun watching the people pass by toward the place where food was being given out. A little girl wrapped in a green cloth went past with a big empty pot on her head. She looked at me, smiled shyly and said, "Hullo, Apu!"

"Hullo, Alia!" I said in reply. Perhaps I hadn't really recovered from my faint. At first I didn't feel at all surprised to recognize one of my little cousins. Then I jumped up and called her back. She stopped and turned round.

"Alia! What are you doing here?" I asked.

"Getting food," she replied, and was about to walk on.

"But how did you get here?"

"In the boat," she said. It was my turn to be asking silly questions and getting odd answers.

"What boat? Who with? Why did you come to this place?" I asked. And now it was Alia who was getting confused and tongue-tied. She was only a young girl, younger than me, and not very bright.

"I came back with Mother and Father and the uncles and aunties," she said. Then she drew the end of her green dress over her head, as even the little girls do when they are shy and confused, and she moved off quickly and joined the crowd that was waiting for food. I was too astonished to follow her before she mixed with the crowd, and once she was among them I couldn't go around looking under all the green headdresses It's not a thing a boy can do.

She had said, "I came back." What could that mean? And what uncles and aunties was she talking about? One of them could be my guardian, Uncle Ahmed, and if I could find him I might—well, I might be able to make myself a real person again, properly written down on paper, instead of a bit of waterweed floating around with the tide. That's what I felt like.

I decided I'd go back and try Mr. Enamel again. I'd ask *him* questions this time. I walked to the office tent, paused at the door, and asked, "May I enter?" as I'd been taught to do at school.

Mr. Enamel's head and spectacles bobbed up over his piles of papers.

"What do you want?" he asked.

"Where's my uncle Ahmed?" I asked.

Mr. Enamel heaved a deep sigh which blew a cloud of dust off the top of the papers.

"Didn't I see you this morning?" he asked.

"Yes," I said. He took a paper from the top of a pile and looked at it.

"You're Apu, otherwise known as Anisuzzaman, son of Bashir?"

"Yes."

"And you're an orphan, in the care of Ahmed, son of Kabir?"

"Yes."

"This morning you said that Ahmed, son of Kabir, was dead."

"Yes."

"And now you want to know where he is?"

"Yes, I've been told he is alive."

The Relief Officer sighed again, hard enough to send a slip of paper floating off the table. I crawled under it, picked up the paper and handed it back.

"I have to inform you," continued Mr. Enamel, "that I have here a statement from Ahmed, son of Kabir, signed with his thumbprint and dated three days ago, certifying that Apu, son of Bashir, is dead."

"Oh," I said. I wasn't sure I understood.

"In other words your uncle has stated that you're dead and you have stated that he's dead."

"I see." I was getting confused again.

"Someone's telling lies round here," said the Relief Officer sternly. "Either he's dead or you're dead. Which is it?"

I was really muddled now. But of course I'd been brought up to believe that grown-ups were always right. I hung my head and said meekly, "It must be me that's dead, sir."

The Relief Officer looked relieved and made a note on the paper. "I'm glad you admit it," he said, smoothing back his smooth hair. "With the Governor coming tomorrow everything's got to be cut and dried." I supposed he was talking about the rice crop—cutting and drying was something I understood. I knew that was important and felt rather ashamed of myself for going around wasting

118

this man's time. As I walked rather sadly out of the tent I turned and saw him looking at me with a puzzled expression on his face. I thought I'd risk one more question.

"If Uncle Ahmed's alive, sir, where is he living?"

"In his *bari*, of course," came the answer from behind the pile of papers.

"I see. Thank you, sir," But I didn't see.

I wandered off round the other tents of the camp. There was a small crowd of island people round the entrance to a dark green tent, so I joined them and peered in. Inside there was one of our people, an old man with white hair, sitting on a box with his back to me, and facing a lot of strangers. There were some city people like Mr. Enamel; a small round man with dark hair and a white pajama but who didn't seem to be one of our people; a very tall man with jute hair cut very short; a man in blue trousers with a lot of black hair and beard; a person in trousers with hair that looked as if a bird had tried to make a nest out of jute, who I decided was a woman; a very thin person with a lot of red hair standing on end, who I decided was a man; a very large person in a long white dress, who must have been a man because he had a beard. I can't remember how many there were altogether or exactly what they looked like but it was no wonder the island people gathered round to stare at the odd collection. I nudged one of the crowd and asked them if the old man was giving them a lesson, but he didn't seem to be too sure who was telling who what.

The strangers were saying things in a language which I could tell was English, and one of the city people was translating it for the white-haired old man. Everyone had something to say and the interpreter had a hard job to keep up with it all. I can't remember who said what, but it all came out something like this:

To make this island safe to live on—
if anyone's to live here at all—
we must keep the numbers small—
we must build a sea wall round the island—
for which we'll need thousands of laborers
we could just build a wall round each village—
or round each *bari*—
perhaps round each cow.

Yes, where will we put the animals?
There are no animals—
We shall bring you animals—
Chickens to lay eggs—
No, eggs to hatch chickens—
Ducks' eggs—

ducks—
and drakes
cows—
and bulls of course—
buffalo cows
(and buffalo bulls)
nannygoats—
and billygoats—

No, goats eat trees!
We need trees—
to break the wind
to break the waves
to shelter the crops
you must grow bananas peanuts pineapples coco-
    nuts betel nuts
more rice more vegetables
we'll give you seeds
seedlings
weedicides
pestilisers
ferticides
fish fry for your tanks—
you'll have more fish to fry!

You must have housing—
bamboo bashas
tinshed roofs
concrete domes

press your own bricks of mud cement and sand
(but there isn't any sand)
You must have shelters
built on stilts
schoolrooms
meeting halls
doctors' dispensaries
somewhere to go when the cyclones come
if anyone's to live on the island at all . . .

After they had talked for a long time they stopped and looked at the old man with white hair and the city man said, "What do you think?"

The old man scratched his white hair, bent his head and neck sideways and said, "Atchha."

The city man translated it into English: "He says O.K."

The old man got up and turned to go. It was my uncle! Not my uncle Ahmed who looked after me but another uncle who had been headman on our island. I greeted him excitedly and he looked at me without much surprise.

"What are you doing here, Uncle?" I asked.

"I am chalking out a plan," he replied with dignity, and walked on.

"Uncle, how can I get food and clothes?"

"That is easy, my boy. Our good friends are giving us not only food and clothes but schools

122

and teachers and boats and I think airplanes as well."

"But they say my name isn't on the paper."

"Ah, of course your name must be on the paper. After that it's easy."

"Can you put my name on the paper, Uncle?"

"My dear child, you know I can't write. But there are plenty of people who can. Go to Mr. Enamel and tell him I sent you." And he walked off in procession with the strangers, talking of jetties and airstrips.

There seemed to be nothing else to do but go back to Mr. Enamel. I paused at the entrance and said, "May I enter?"

His eyes bobbed up and looked at me. "What do you want?" he asked.

"I want to get on the paper."

"Oh, it's you again," he said. "You'll have to go back where you came from. Where do you come from?"

"I come from Kukuri Mukuri Char," I said.

"Well, you'll have to go back there." He disappeared behind his papers. I wandered toward the door. Before I got there he stopped me.

"Where did you say you came from?" he demanded.

"Kukuri Mukuri Char."

"Impossible," he said.

I stood still for a bit, but I couldn't let it go at that. I asked, "Why is it impossible, sir?"

"Because this is Kukuri Mukuri Char," he said flatly.

I thought about this for a bit. Then I said respectfully, "I beg your pardon, sir, but *that* is impossible."

"Why is it impossible?" he asked crossly.

"Because I come from there and it's not like this."

He got quite angry. "First you say you're dead. Now you say you come from Kukuri Mukuri Char when in fact you've come *to* Kukuri Mukuri Char. You're wasting my time."

I went out feeling sad and more muddled than ever. Not only was I dead and with nowhere to go, but I hadn't even come from the place I'd come from.

I was glad to meet Khoka outside the tent. He looked at me and said, "What's the matter? Have you seen a ghost?"

"No," I answered. "But I think I *am* one." I told him what the Relief Officer had said to me. He thumped me on the back and said, "Don't worry about him! All these people who can read and write are the same. It gets them muddled. Come and meet these people I've met. They say I can join their family. Perhaps they'll take you as well."

It was late in the evening as I followed him across the fields, over a creek by a new bamboo bridge and toward a cluster of *bari* huts on a mound. The red sun was going down over the paddy and our long shadows stretched toward a clump of trees with fresh green leaves shining on the battered branches. I saw that what I'd thought to be huts were in fact tents. But if they had been huts, and if there had been more trees, and more branches on the trees that were standing, it would have looked quite like my old *bari*. Again I had that strange peaceful feeling of coming home. I felt it but I didn't of course believe it.

I felt shy of going to this strange family and asking if I could join them. Khoka said there was nothing to be afraid of. They'd lost some of their own people and were glad to adopt him. But then Khoka was quite shameless, and used to pushing himself where he mightn't be wanted.

I hung back outside the *bari* and told him to go ahead and speak for me. The whole place reminded me so much of my old home that I was almost in tears again. Khoka told me not to be so soft, but he agreed to go in and ask.

He was quite a long time gone. I sat at the bottom of the *bari* mound and watched the sun dip behind the trees. Khoka came out, looking embarrassed.

"They say they can only take one boy of my

125

age, in place of one who disappeared. They'll pretend I'm him. They say they'll get me on the papers, but they can't do it twice. Come on in though. They'll give you a bed for the night, I'm sure."

I thought I'd better go back to the hospital tent, where at least I was on a list. I didn't want just another bed for the night. But Khoka persuaded me and dragged me up the mound and round the tents, which stood with their backs to the outside world just as the huts had done.

Sitting in front of the tent was my Uncle Ahmed.

Tape 10:
GOVERNOR VISITS
KUKURI MUKURI

The evening had been almost like the good old days, but not quite. I had been surrounded by the faces of the family I knew, but too many were missing, and there were strangers, distant relations from other islands who had joined the *bari*. Of course I listened to their stories of how they had survived the cyclone on floating logs and the bottoms of upturned boats. Then I had told mine. They had listened with open mouths as I tried to explain about aircraft carriers and hotels, but somehow I had found it difficult to believe in myself.

We had eaten a family meal, but there was not very much food and some of the strange members of the family had muttered about the two extra mouths to feed—that was Khoka and myself, who weren't on the ration list for free food.

Then we had slept—the first time I had slept properly in a cozy family *bari* for what seemed a lifetime. Though I was very tired, I had lain awake for some time when the others had gone to sleep, and the feeling of homecoming had flowed over me. In spite of the flapping of the tent in the breeze the other night sounds seemed to be just as I remembered them: the breathing of other sleepers, the whisper of leaves, the wash of water in the creek and on the nearby shore.

I woke feeling that I'd slept for a week. The sun was only just beginning to light up the tent, but the family members were doing their morning things: cleaning their teeth with bits of twig, spitting, going down to the creek to wash, preparing a simple breakfast.

I found there was still a thought that was troubling me. My uncle was kneeling in the sun, saying his morning prayer. When he had finished I went up to him and said, "Uncle, when are we going back to Kukuri Mukuri?"

He looked at me very strangely and at last said, "This *is* Kukuri Mukuri, my boy."

I ran to one of the trees that were left, felt its trunk, climbed into the lower branches and looked at the knobs and stumps on it. I was satisfied. There couldn't be another tree exactly like that in the world. The shape of the island might be changed, the course of the creek might alter, great trees might be carried away, but I could recognize the fork in the branches where I'd sat— when I was a child, I was going to say. Anyway it seemed to have been in another life.

I was home, with my family, but the *bari* was still a borrowed tent and the family was still being fed from the relief camp. My uncle said he would take me down to the office tent and put the papers straight.

"What about Khoka?" I said.

"We offered him your place in the family," my uncle said. "He can't have that now we know you're alive. But one day we shall need young men to work the land. If that's what he wants to do we must try to fit him in."

Did Khoka want to spend his days growing rice? I doubted it, but I said nothing. After all, if it hadn't been for him I wouldn't have found my way home.

There seemed to be a lot going on when we got to the camp. The tents were arranged on the sides of a big square, and this was being cleared of stores and some men were arranging a sort of platform of crates at one end. The village people were already lining up for food, but a soldier was saying to them, "You'll have to wait till the Governor comes."

We went to the office tent. Mr. Enamel was busier than ever checking lists and sorting papers. He didn't even look up when my uncle asked permission to enter, but just said, "Well, what is it?"

"Ahmed, son of Kabir, and Apu, son of Bashir," my uncle said.

"I remember you two," said Mr. Enamel, still without looking up. "Have you made up your minds which one of you's dead?"

"Respected Sir," said my uncle politely. "I wish to state there's been an error."

"No time for errors today," snapped Mr. Enamel. "The Governor's coming to inspect the relief work and everything's got to be in order. Come back tomorrow."

Following my uncle, I once again walked toward the door of the tent. Before I got there Mr. Enamel said, "Would you like to be useful?"

I'd no idea how anyone could be useful among all that paper, but my uncle thought quicker than me and gave me a push. Then I thought that if I was useful he might change his mind about my being dead, so I waited.

Mr. Enamel said, "Carry all these papers to

the table outside." I set to work, blowing dust and spiders off stacks of paper, carrying them out to a table by the side of the square, and arranging them neatly in stacks again as the Relief Officer directed.

"Are they valuable, all those papers?" I asked him as I collected a pile.

He seemed quite pleased to talk about his work. "Of course they're valuable," he said. "On those papers are every man, woman and child born on the island; every *bari* and hut; every square inch of land and who possesses it; every cow, buffalo and goat; every boat. Everything there was before the cyclone and everything that was left afterward. And of course every blanket, every *lungi,* every spoonful of milk powder, every grain of rice we have given away. If we lost these papers all this valuable knowledge would be gone."

Though I knew I couldn't read I looked at the paper on the top of the stack. The writing looked like strips of washing flapping on a line. There was nothing that looked like a *bari,* a buffalo or a boat.

"How did you find all this out, sir?" I asked him.

"By *research,* my child. That is, by asking people a great number of questions."

I thought about this as I trotted out with an-

131

other pile. When I came back for more I asked him, "Do you only ask questions of people who know a lot?"

He laughed at this. "No," he said. "We get our information from very ignorant people, like yourself. But it isn't *knowledge* until it's written down."

As I made another journey to the table outside I thought to myself: *So that's it. Clever people have knowledge: ignorant people only know things.* I knew I was alive. But it wasn't knowledge until it was written down.

It was at that moment, pausing at the door of the tent, that I saw there was room for improvement in written-down knowledge. It was wrong about me being dead; it might be wrong about other things. I suppose I might have decided that knowledge was no good, but from that moment I decided I would learn to read and write sometime, and do something about it.

All round the edge of the square people were arranging things. There was only one table, the one with Mr. Enamel's papers on it, but there were boxes and crates and piles of sacks and stacks of tins, and all over them were arranged papers and pictures and charts and maps like the ones they used to stick on the walls of the classrooms at school. The strange people with the different sorts of hair that I'd seen yesterday were doing most of the arranging.

I walked round and looked at the papers. Some of them were easy to understand. There were pictures of beautiful ears of rice, and I was told this meant we could grow more rice. There were pictures of handsome chickens, and I was told this meant we could raise more chickens. There was a picture of a smiling family with two healthy children. I said to the tall man who was pinning it up, "That means we must have more children, doesn't it?" He didn't speak my language very well, and I must have misunderstood his reply. I thought he said we should have *fewer* children, but I probably got it wrong. The rest of the papers were writing and things I didn't understand at all.

I walked past the crates that were arranged like the platform we used to have at school, past a collection of odd teacups and mugs, and past the line of people still waiting patiently for food. One or two of them I recognized as people from the village on the other side of the island, but most of them were complete strangers. They said they had come here to work.

I found it very difficult to believe that all these strange faces and all these stiff tents were on my quiet island of Kukuri Mukuri Char. The only thing that wasn't strange was the water that showed through the gaps between the tents, sparkling in the sun as it flowed toward the sea.

People kept looking at the sky, and almost every sentence anyone spoke in any language contained the word "helicopter." I didn't have to ask what was going to happen. They were expecting the Governor to arrive by helicopter, and it seemed that it was going to land in the middle of the square.

People stopped scurrying about with papers. Everything seemed ready. The foreigners fidgeted, smoked cigarettes, and kept looking at their wristwatches. The villagers and workers, though they'd had no food, squatted patiently.

A girl suddenly pointed and shouted, "Airplane!" All the heads turned. But it was a vulture. We all became quiet again. It was silent except for the wash of the water on the shore.

I was the first to see it—I know a helicopter when I see one. It was quite high above the horizon and we couldn't hear the noise yet. I just pointed, and all the heads turned again.

The noise of the chopper grew louder, and it came wandering toward us as if looking for the right place to land. Soon it was hanging in the sky over our heads. The soldiers stood to attention, Mr. Enamel straightened his tie, and the nurse began pouring out cups of tea.

The helicopter started dropping downward. It swooped quite quickly at first and then when it was just above the tent tops it seemed to send out a great gust of wind to stop itself from falling.

A gust? It was a baby cyclone. A great cloud of dust, straw and leaves swirled into the air. I saw the nurse holding her headdress on and trying to cover the cups to keep the dust out. The charts and pictures took off from all the boxes and circled, flapping into the air like vultures. The tents themselves were falling flat all round us or leaping about like maddened cows. And every single paper on Mr. Enamel's table, bearing the name of every single man, woman, child, *bari*, cow, buffalo, goat, and boat on the island, all went fluttering away over the paddy fields toward the water. Beyond the flattened tents we could see them settling one by one like seabirds onto the dancing waves and beginning their voyage on the current toward the open sea. Mr. Enamel watched, unbelieving, as all his weeks of work flew away. Then he covered his face with his hands. I think he was crying.

At last the whirling blades of the helicopter stopped. The door opened and a man jumped out and fixed some steps. The first man to come out was one of the photographers who had come when I'd been all alone on the island. He turned to take a picture of the Governor coming down the steps.

Then he faced the flattened tents, among which people were struggling with ropes and poles and chasing after flapping papers, and coolly took pictures of the disorder.

The Governor looked around him. "Have you had some more wind?" he asked.

Tape 11:
CROCODILES AND
TIGERS

The pleasant sunny days of winter are passing away and the spring weather's getting so hot and dry that we'd normally be looking forward to the dark, wet days of summer.

(You say that's going to look funny when it's translated? Well, I can't help it.)

We're all rather worried about whether the houses will be built before the rains begin. We don't much care what they're made of as long as they keep the rain out. The camp's gone, and the soldiers and the foreigners and most of the paper, and we've sowed seeds and we're waiting for the next crop. Oh, no, they haven't forgotten us. They sent us seeds and animals and fishing nets and things, and we get enough food to keep us going. And we've got more water than we ever used to have at this time of year. They've made us a deep tube well. They kept driving these big metal pipes into the soil, and slushing out the mud, and then they fitted a motor pump onto it and it soon began to pump up clear water, from hundreds of feet below, they said.

It doesn't taste of anything, this water, and the old people say it can't do you much good, but we're getting used to it. Khoka's the one who was most interested in the tube well. He'd tried his hand at sowing and planting out rice, and carrying water for the seedlings, but he hadn't the patience to wait for them to grow. As soon as they started sinking the well he began to hang about the place. I think he had some idea to begin with that they were looking for oil, and he'd heard that finding oil was a good way to get rich quick. Actually oil's the problem. The motor pump works on oil and unless the oil comes in the boats we get no water.

But still, the idea of getting something for nothing appealed to Khoka, even if it was only water. So now he's the assistant to the man who runs the pump. They are making a lot of little channels for watering the paddy fields, and Khoka helps to see that every field gets its fair share. It seems to keep him happy and I hope he'll decide to settle down on the island.

I noticed that another place where Khoka was hanging around quite a lot was the jetty they've built for landing stores from the boats. I met him down there one day and asked him why he was there every time a boat came in. I was afraid he was thinking of getting a lift away from the island, but he said it wasn't that. When I asked him what it was he just said, "They may come for me."

I had forgotten what he'd told me on the cargo boat coming down to Tazumuddin—that the gang had sent him down there and they'd follow him up to see how much he was making out of it. But I could see that he was worried.

I said, "Let them take their share of water. Those city beggars could do with a wash!" But he still looked gloomy and said they would come and take him away. I was sorry to see him unhappy, just when things seemed to be going well on the island, and I was glad when he took up sea fishing as a hobby.

We had been given a boat to replace the ones sunk by the cyclone, but it was a foreign one made of metal and nobody liked it except Khoka. He took to rowing out in it, with a line and hooks—

a way of fishing we had not used on the island before. Sometimes I went with him, and I did my best to teach him about the tides and tell him when it was safe to go and when it wasn't. He still didn't exactly *approve* of the tides, but he had stopped fighting them.

Of course the big thing that's going on here now is that they are building a school. A load of fine new bricks arrived at the jetty, and most of the village turned out to land them. But you'll never guess what we did to those bricks. We smashed them all up! Nobody would believe it at first when they gave us hammers and told us to break all those beautiful bricks to pieces. But they said it had to be done, and Khoka, as usual, was the first to try this new game. One bang and you had two half-bricks—just the size to throw at a policeman Khoka said, but I hoped he wouldn't start that here. Then each half had to be broken into smaller pieces and each piece pounded into bits the size of your fingernail. After a time even Khoka got tired of breaking things, but we had to go on until we had a mountain of chipped brick. Then they landed loads of gray cement powder in paper sacks, and we were shown how to mix it with the bricks and water and sand—the sand had to come in boats too—and they said the mixture would go as hard as—well, as hard as bricks,

I suppose. Somehow I felt sorry for the people who had gone to all the trouble to make the bricks in the first place.

(Do you have to do this in your country? What's that? You pick up little stones off the beach or out of the ground? Well, they say yours is a rich country.)

Meanwhile we had meetings about the new school. We decided that the little children will go to school in the mornings, and the older ones like me in the afternoons and the grown-ups in the evenings when they have finished their work. It will be a race to see who learns their ABCs first.

Of course I was the only boy on the island who'd been to school before, so they asked me what I thought about education. Pretty boring stuff if you can't read or write, I was going to say, but that sounded a bit rude so I said I thought we ought to have some. And the next thing was that they asked me to be Head Boy! Me—Apu, who'd lived like a mouse in a hole on that empty island that—no, it couldn't have been the same place as Kukuri Mukuri Char, with its tube well and its jetty and its two-storied school.

I said I wouldn't mind being Head Boy. *The Head Boy at the school in the city had a moustache!* They actually wrote it on a paper—oh yes, we had the teacher there already—Head Boy, Anisuzzaman. One day I shall be able to read it for myself.

I came out from the meeting and I wanted to tell my good news to Khoka. I looked by the pump. He wasn't there. I went down to the jetty. He wasn't there either and the metal dinghy was gone. It was getting dark and I could see that the tide was running rapidly out to sea. I waited by the jetty until dark and the boat didn't come back. I went slowly back to the *bari,* and I was so worried about Khoka that I forgot to tell my uncle about being made Head Boy.

Khoka wants to tell the next bit himself, so he may as well do the talking.

I can't tell stories like Apu but I'll say what happened. I went out in the boat. I knew the tide was going to change so I went north, toward the mainland. There I was alone in the boat and I hooked this big *bekti.* That's a fish. I know it was a *bekti* because I did get it into the boat in the end. I was trying to get it in when this launch came past.

It was a small launch with clean white paint and its engines sounded powerful. The sort of boat the *sahibs* go around in. It drove past me and rocked my little boat just as I was trying to grab the fish, so I turned and swore at them. The launch

142

came round in a circle and a man leaned out of it and called, "Which way to Kukuri Mukuri Char?"

I didn't feel much like helping them anyhow, but I was just going to point to the island when I saw something that made me stop and think. I recognized Bhuiyan sitting in the launch. I'd seen him often enough in the city. He had skin all roughened by smallpox and a lot of big teeth like a crocodile. He'd been pointed out to me in the streets, sometimes walking among the crowds in a pajama or even in a *lungi*, sometimes riding in a big car with a driver, like a *sahib*. Bhuiyan was one of the gang leaders who make the money out of beggars. There he was now, sitting in trousers and shirt like a *sahib* going on a picnic.

I was pretty sure he didn't know me. But why should he be going to Kukuri Mukuri? There was only one reason. The gang had sent me down there, and now he was following up to see what the pickings were like.

I pretended to be busy with the fish in the bottom of the boat, so they couldn't see my face. I wasn't sure who else was in the launch. It came right alongside my little boat, and even bumped it so that I nearly fell overboard. I could see the faces of all the five men in the boat now, and there didn't seem to be anyone there who would know me.

They asked me again, "Which way to Kukuri Mukuri?" What to do? I was quite sure I didn't want any of these men on the island. Why should they come and spoil things? But if I said I didn't know where Kukuri Mukuri was they might go over to the island and ask for themselves. So I pointed toward the sun—it was nearly setting—and said, "Kukuri Mukuri's that way. A long way."

The man who'd spoken first asked me if they'd get there by dark. I thought if I said no they'd go for the nearest land, which *was* Kukuri Mukuri So I twisted my shoulders as if I wasn't sure and said, "Maybe."

There was some talk among the men in the cabin and then the man said, "How do you know where Kukuri Mukuri is?" I made a mistake then. I said, "Because I come from there."

So they said, "Get in the launch. We'll take you back."

I said, "What about my boat?" They told me to tie it on behind and they'd tow it.

There was nothing I could do. We tied the boat on and I got into the cabin. It was more like an airplane or a motorcar than a boat. It had a steering wheel and clocks and things. The driver pulled a lever and the engines roared, the nose of the launch lifted and we shot ahead. It would have been great if I'd known where we were going and what was going to happen.

The five men in the launch were the driver, his helper (who I'd been talking to), Bhuiyan, and two other dark men who were talking with him on the seat in the cabin. My only idea was to get them as far away from Kukuri Mukuri as I could, but I didn't know how much they knew.

"The *sahibs* have a paper of the island?" I asked the boatman.

He said, "If they had a map we wouldn't need you, fisherboy. You stink of fish."

"But they have skillful pilots who know the islands?" I said. I pretended not to notice the insult.

"You don't think we're island fishermen, do you?" the boatman said. "We drive the *sahibs* up and down the river to Narayanganj."

I knew I had them then. They knew less about the islands than I did. It wouldn't be difficult to get them lost.

They had no idea who I was, either. Bhuiyan and the other two men ignored me and went on talking in low voices. Or rather it was Bhuiyan who did most of the talking, and the other two agreed with him all the time. Every now and then I could hear bits of what he was saying.

" . . . fishermen! They've got webbed feet and they're giving them Italian shoes!"

145

" . . . all those medicines. You know what some of those drugs sell for, if we can get them back to the city . . ."

" . . . too healthy as they are. Not a useful cripple in the islands . . ."

" . . . need to bring more of our beggars down here. Rotten beggars, these peasants . . ."

"You say you sent a kid down weeks ago? He should be able to show us around by now . . . how old? . . too young to know much and too old to beg, unless he's blind or something . . . yes, I know we could fix that . . ."

The hairs prickled on the back of my neck when I knew they were talking about me. Should be able to show them around, should I? I'd show them!

We drove toward the sunset. It was about high tide, I think, which was why we got over the mudbanks. Bits of shore kept coming into view, but I kept saying, "Not that one. Not that one. Round the next headland."

Soon the sun was a round red ball sitting on a fringe of trees. Bhuiyan looked at a big gold watch on his wrist and spoke to me for the first time. "Aren't we there yet?"

"The *sahib* need not worry," I said. "The hospitality of the islands awaits him."

I got out of the cabin and stood on the side

146

of the launch. The land ahead looked very wild: all trees, no open fields, no sign of *baris*. I didn't like the look of it myself.

I jumped down into the cabin and spoke to Bhuiyan. "That's Kukuri Mukuri ahead. The sahib would like to be taken to the commander of the army?" I knew that would scare him.

"I wouldn't like to disturb him this evening," Bhuiyan said. "Show us a quiet anchorage for the night."

An anchorage didn't suit the plan I had for them. "Tides are very strong here, *sahib*. Better to go ashore for the night. I will show you a private spot." It all looked pretty private to me.

They agreed, so just as the sun dipped behind the trees I told the driver to turn up a creek running inland. Dense jungle trees hung over on each side. Their roots were like long, thin fingers. The driver slowed down the engine and we chugged quietly up the creek. Jungle noises came at us from each side.

Bhuiyan looked at the jungle, then at me. "Are you sure this is Kukuri Mukuri?" he demanded.

"Of course, *sahib*," I answered. "Welcome to my island!" I wished I was a thousand miles away from it.

As we passed a mudbank a log crawled off it on legs and slid with a splash into the water.

"What's that?" Bhuiyan gasped. Somebody exclaimed, "Crocodile!"

Of course I'd never seen one before but I said, "*Sahib* would like a very nice crocodile skin? Make very fine shoes, handbags. *Sahib* is here for the hunting?"

You old crocodile, I felt like saying to him. *Your skin's as thick and your teeth are as big and your face is as ugly. This mudbank's where you belong.*

The boatman asked me where the landing place was. I saw a fairly clear stretch of bank running down to a mudflat and told him to steer for that. He asked if it was all right and I said, "Of course. It's low water; next tide will float you off." I thought in fact that it was a little past high water. As I guessed, the driver was only an ignorant townee, and he believed me.

We grounded on the mud. The boatman went to the front of the boat. They were going to jump ashore, but the bank seemed to be lined with spikes growing upward out of the mud. It didn't look very welcoming.

They managed to land, and they collected some wood and made a fire. They took my *bekti* fish and cooked it; but they didn't offer to pay for it. It wasn't a very jolly party, and soon afterward we settled down for the night. Bhuiyan and the other two men shared the cabin. One of them

148

must have been on the floor, because there were only two benches. The boatmen were sent out to the foredeck. I pulled the dinghy up and got into it.

My plan had been to get away in the dinghy and leave them to it, but I had no idea where I was and I didn't feel like going off on my own in the dark. So I curled up in the dinghy for the night.

The night seemed very long. The jungle sizzled with insects, and strange calls came out of it which might have been birds, beasts or demons. Frogs shouted into my ears from the mud. Strange blue lights flashed in the trees.

Of course the tide in the creek ran out and the launch gradually heeled over on the mud. There was a thump and a lot of curses, which must have been Bhuiyan rolling off the bench on to the other man, and at about the same time the boatmen found themselves sliding off the foredeck and woke up screaming about crocodiles.

I wasn't too happy myself, though my little dinghy was on a level keel. I dozed off and had a funny dream about cats in a black alley, and when I woke up I thought I could still smell cat. I stared hard into the darkness and the harder I stared at each jungle bush the more it seemed to walk around. But nothing seemed to be happening and I suppose all six of us went to sleep again.

At dawn we were all awake. There was a cold, clammy mist and I was shivering. The men were leaning out of the launch and, with a lot of bad language, asking me when the water would come back. I said it would be all right in an hour or two, but I don't think they believed me this time. One of Bhuiyan's men jumped off on to the mud and came toward me threateningly. Then he looked down at his feet and let out an oath.

Then I saw what he'd seen. Ever seen the footprints left by a pussycat in a bit of wet cement? There were footprints like that all over the mud— *only each print was as big as a fair-sized cat!*

I don't think any of us had seen anything like it before but we all said the same thing at once— *tiger!*

Bhuiyan began roaring at everyone, "Where d'you think you've brought me? I haven't come down here to be eaten by tigers! Get me out of here! Get me back to the city!"

I moved quicker than I've ever moved, even in city traffic. I let go of the boat rope, shoved the boat over the mud into the water, climbed in, grabbed the oars and pulled away down the creek as fast as I could row. Bhuiyan yelled, "Stop him!" and the man started wading into the water with the idea of swimming after me. Then he stopped. I knew what he was thinking. Crocodiles!

Rowing backward, I could see Bhuiyan leaping out of the launch and running to the water's edge with something in his hand. There was a BANG!— a lot of birds flew out of the trees and something came skipping over the water at me. He fired the pistol again and another bullet skipped past. Then I was round a bend in the creek and beyond his reach.

I heard him shouting that he would give me a lot of money if I would come back. He should have thought of that before he started shooting.

I'm not going to tell you how I got back to Kukuri Mukuri. It took about a week, getting lifts in country boats. Poor old Apu was quite glad to see me when I turned up on a load of bricks.

Am I sorry for Bhuiyan and the men, stuck down there with the tigers and the crocodiles? No, I'm sorry for the tigers and crocodiles.

Do I want to stay on Kukuri Mukuri Char? Well, I've got to get the place fixed up for the next cyclone.

ABOUT THE AUTHOR

Clive King is the author of a number of acclaimed books for young readers, including *Me and My Million,* which was a *Boston Globe/Horn Book* Honor Book and a *School Library Journal* Best Book 1979.

Born in Richmond (Surrey), England, Mr. King studied at Cambridge University. He worked abroad for many years, primarily in the Mideast and Asia. "I lived in Dacca (then East Pakistan) for four years, working for their Education Directorate," he writes. "Like most westerners I was almost overwhelmed by the poverty, disease, and insoluble economic problems. . . . I couldn't see how a children's story could possibly arise from the misery of the Bengali people, yet oddly enough it was a great disaster that triggered it off. I was there in November 1970 when the cyclonic wave in the Ganges delta drowned over a million people in one night. I joined a makeshift relief expedition, thirty people of all races, aboard a ramshackle Ganges boat with one toilet, and we were down there for ten days among the devastation, floating bodies, starving survivors, and fear of epidemics to follow. Thus, of all my books, *The Night the Water Came* is most concerned with truth of experience."

Mr. King and his wife now live in Thurlton (Norfolk), England. He has three children.